Emma and Luke are Totally Together

RACHEL ARNETT

Copyright © 2019 by Rachel Arnett

All rights reserved.

This is a work of fiction. Names, characters, businesses, places, events, locales, and incidents are either the products of the author's imagination or used in a fictitious manner. Any resemblance to actual persons, living or dead, or actual events is purely coincidental.

No part of this book may be reproduced in any form or by any electronic or mechanical means, including information storage and retrieval systems, without written permission from the author, except for the use of brief quotations in a book review.

ISBN: 9781079137187

1

THE MOST IMPORTANT thing is for the marshmallow to be on top.

"And by that, I mean the *whole* marshmallow," says Sherrie, our manager. "A cut or nibbled one will disqualify your team."

"You hear that?" I whisper to Luke. "No nibbling the marshmallow."

Luke shoots me an incredulous look that says, *Who, me?*

It's early on a Thursday morning, and we—all forty-two employees of Artisanal Goods, a purveyor of, you guessed it, artisanal goods—have been summoned into the conference room for some good old fashioned team building. Sherrie has a thing for team building exercises. We do them far more often than necessary. I guess that's Sherrie's prerogative, though. And I do have to admit that I'm intrigued by today's activity—something called the Marshmallow Challenge.

As Sherrie does a lap around the conference room, dividing us into groups with gestures of her hand, she finishes going over the rules: we must construct our structure with the provided materials only; we are not allowed to suspend our structure to another object; we are permitted to rebuild our structure as many times as we like until the timer goes off; aside from the marshmallow, we may alter our materials in any way.

"The team that builds the tallest structure wins," Sherrie says, beaming with excitement. "You have eighteen minutes, starting now."

I take a moment to consider my teammates. Thankfully, Luke and I have been put into the same group. We've been friends since I started working at Artisanal Goods six years ago; we clicked right away. Luke is down-to-earth, a hard worker, an all-around good guy. And, objectively, I'm aware of the fact that he's handsome. The dude is in shape, too, thanks to all the recreational rugby he plays. But he's nothing more than a friend.

The guy I daydream about? That would be Alex, also a coworker. Alex is…well, he's mega handsome. Need I say more? Unfortunately for me, though, mega handsome Alex is on the opposite side of the room right now.

Also in our group is Derek—a nice guy, if a bit oblivious. I feel neither glad nor annoyed that Derek is on our team. It's our fourth member, Paige, whom I'm already gritting my teeth about.

Where do I even start with Paige? She gets too close to you when she talks. She has a habit of reciting the weirdest facts. She's always leaving unpalatable home-cooked goods in the break room and pestering everyone to try them.

I open up the bag that Sherrie gave us and empty its contents onto the floor. Our provided materials are as follows: one perfectly puffy marshmallow, three feet of string, three feet of painter's tape, and twenty strands of uncooked spaghetti.

"This should be interesting," says Luke.

"Did Sherrie say we can or can't cut up the marshmallow?" asks Derek.

"The marshmallow must stay whole, Derek," I say.

Paige picks up the little bundle of spaghetti, brings it to her nose, and gives it an intense sniff.

"Mmm," she says.

A small part of me wants to ask what she can possibly tell from smelling the uncooked spaghetti. But mostly I don't want to know.

For the first half of our allotted time, our team of four discusses what our spaghetti structure should look like. We debate whether we should double up the spaghetti or not. We debate whether we should break the spaghetti into smaller pieces. And then we debate about the best way to use the string and tape, and whether we actually need to use the string at all.

"Fun fact," says Paige. "The first violin strings were made from dried sheep intestines."

I ignore her. "We shouldn't use the string if we don't need it."

"I agree," says Luke.

"Maybe we're not supposed to use the *tape?*" suggests Derek.

Luke glances at the clock up on the conference room wall, and then around at the other teams.

"We better start building, you guys," he says.

And so we do. We tape. We construct. We quickly but efficiently assemble our spaghetti structure. Six minutes later, there's three minutes left and all we have left to do is add the pièce de résistance.

We turn to Derek, who has been safeguarding the marshmallow in his palm. He nods and swallows. It's his big moment. It's all up to him now. Carefully, so carefully, he uses his other hand to pick up the marshmallow from his palm and transfer it to the top of our tower. He presses it down onto the ends of the taped-together spaghetti, piercing the soft little pillow, deforming it slightly as he secures it in place. Finally, as we draw a collective breath in, Derek moves his hand away.

For exactly three seconds, our structure stands proud. It's majestic. It's glorious. I've never seen a more beautiful thing. Behold, the great spaghetti tower! Oh, what a sight it is.

And then—and I swear, it's like it happens in theatric slow motion—the whole thing collapses.

Spaghetti strand after spaghetti strand, our tower breaks apart. Meanwhile, the marshmallow somehow dislodges itself and comes tumbling down. It rolls along the carpet, coming to a stop right by the toe of my shoe. In that moment, it becomes obvious that we've made a fatal mistake: we underestimated the weight of the marshmallow.

The four of us stand there, in silent dismay, for what feels like an eternity.

Finally, Luke speaks up.

"We need a stronger base," he says.

Immediately, his comment gets my own thoughts churning.

"Triangles," I exclaim.

Luke snaps and points a finger gun at me.

"*Yes*," he says. "Good thinking, Armstrong."

As we scramble to reassemble our spaghetti strands into triangles, I can't help but think about how good of a team Luke and I make. How in sync we always are. How things get done when we put our heads together.

And that's when the idea comes to me.

I know how I'm going to fix my Hawaii problem.

TO EXPLAIN, I need to back up a little—by twelve hours, to be exact, to the Skype chat I had with my family the night before. The call consisted of my older sister Catherine (the golden child, the environmental lawyer), my younger brother Garrett (the chill college student), our parents (sweet old Dad and always generous Mom), and, of course, yours truly. Mom and Dad still live in the house we all grew up in, but the rest of us live in other cities now, so most of our face-to-face interaction these days is facilitated via the wonders of technology.

The purpose of the video chat was to figure out where we wanted to go on our annual June vacation together. June is the slowest time of year for Mom and Dad's restaurant, so we always schedule our family vacations then. This year, however, the planning was happening more last minute than usual.

We'd originally scheduled the chat for weeks earlier, but then things kept coming up for Catherine that she apparently couldn't reschedule, and by the time we all actually connected, there were only a few weeks left until June. Nobody except for me seemed annoyed by this, though. Like I said, Catherine's the golden child. She could set her own house on fire and the rest of our family would say, "Well, she must have had a good reason for doing it."

Everyone else was already signed on when I joined the chat. Mom and Dad's faces filled up the upper left quadrant of my laptop screen. In the space below them, Garrett was sitting at his desk in his cramped off-campus apartment. Catherine had called in from her living room in San Francisco; I could practically see a view of the Golden Gate Bridge over her shoulder.

Catherine was in the midst of telling everyone about the case she was working on—something that sounded dismal, as usual.

"I mean, can you imagine?" Catherine was saying. "A *hundred thousand tons* of the stuff. And it's extraordinarily toxic, of course. It's like these people have no conscience."

"Well, we're proud of you for trying to do something about it," Mom said.

Catherine shrugged. "I do what I can."

I let the moment of reflective silence pass, then waved at the screen and said, "Hey, guys."

"Oh, Emma," Mom said. "I didn't see you log on. Well, at any rate. Now that we're all here, should we discuss the trip?"

"Where do *you* want to go, Mom?" asked Catherine, her tone instantly perking up. "Dad?"

"Oh, anywhere is fine," said Dad, smiling and shrugging.

"Someplace tropical would be nice," said Mom.

"Like Hawaii?" asked Catherine.

I adjusted my laptop screen. "We were there two years ago," I pointed out. "What about someplace new?"

"We would go to a different island," said Catherine, as if that was more than obvious. "Garrett? What do you think?"

In his corner of the screen, Garrett nodded. "Hawaii's cool."

"Great," said Catherine. "How about Maui this time?"

"Maui sounds *lovely*," said Mom.

"What about—" I started to say.

But Catherine interrupted me. "Perfect. And since you two have a big anniversary coming up, I'd like to plan the trip."

"Oh, you don't have to do that, Catherine," said Dad.

"I'd like to, though," said Catherine.

"Well...if you really want to," said Mom.

"I insist," said Catherine.

"Guess that's settled, then," I said, picking at a stain on my jeans.

"Actually, there is one more thing." Catherine glanced off-screen. "Honey? Can you come over here?"

As soon as Catherine asked her husband to join her, I knew what was about to happen. My sister has never been subtle about her desire to have kids. Even when we were kids ourselves, she used to run around declaring that she was going to have two boys and two girls—all perfectly staggered in age, of course.

Sure enough, as soon as Kenneth sat down and waved hello to the rest of us, Catherine hooked her arm through his and smiled at us giddily.

"We thought about holding off until the trip to share this," she said. "But we just can't wait."

"Catherine," gasped Mom. "Are you—"

Catherine nodded. "Pregnant!"

Mom shrieked with delight. Dad laughed and hugged Mom. It was along the lines of the reaction they'd had back when Catherine and Kenneth announced their engagement, only turned up a notch. Okay, more like half a dozen notches.

Both Garrett and I congratulated Catherine and Kenneth, but Mom's excitement continued to dominate the screen.

"That is absolutely the best news," Mom said, delicately wiping away tears. "How wonderful, you two. How *wonderful*."

And with that, Catherine officially confirmed her place as the favorite daughter. After all, how could I compete with someone growing a human being?

Five minutes later, the call was over, and I was left feeling all sorts of stupid feelings: inadequacy, bitterness, irritation with myself for feeling that way in the first place. And I couldn't help but dread our upcoming family vacation. I mean, I always dreaded our vacations a little; no Armstrong family gathering was complete without me feeling lousy about my lack of a relationship or meaningful career. But now I dreaded it like the bubonic plague. I imagined every conversation revolving around Catherine and Kenneth's impending little marvel; I imagined Mom endlessly repeating how wonderful it was. Nobody would say outright how pitiful my own life was in comparison, but the implication—oh, no doubt about it—the implication would be there.

Sad little Emma. The twenty-eight-year-old apple of no one's eye. Doomed to the cubicle forever.

THERE ARE BARELY two minutes left on the clock when Luke, Derek, Paige, and I start to reconstruct our spaghetti tower. Maniacally, we strip the tape off our strands of spaghetti and re-tape them into triangles. We work quickly, mutely, utterly focused on the task at hand.

But time waits for no spaghetti constructor.

And so we don't win the Marshmallow Challenge. We don't even come close. But I emerge from the conference room that morning with pep in my step anyway, because I've won something even better: a solution to my own little problem.

A few hours post-team-building-exercise, I send Luke a chat message on my computer: *Want to grab coffee?*

Sure, he types back. *Just let me wrap something up.*

Five minutes, an elevator ride, and a block-and-a-half-walk later, we're strolling into The Brilliant Bean. The café is crowded that afternoon. The room is humming with the collective buzz of caffeine, and at first glance, it appears as if all of the tables are taken.

Then I spot one open beside the condiment bar, and we grab it as soon as we get our coffees.

"So my annual family vacation is coming up," I say, taking a seat.

"Oh yeah?" says Luke. "Where are you guys off to this year?"

I pantomime hula arms.

"What is that? Are you doing *Thriller*?"

"You know what I'm doing."

Luke grins. "So, Hawaii. Nice."

"Have you ever been?" I ask.

Luke shakes his head. "Nope. Always wanted to, though."

It's almost like it's meant to be.

I *am* a tad nervous, though. Just a little. It's not as if I've asked anything like this of Luke before, and I'm well aware of the ridiculousness of my forthcoming request. Buying a few seconds to collect myself, I pop off the lid of my coffee and let some steam billow out.

"You excited to go?" asks Luke.

"Yes and no," I say. "I'm excited for the island. I'm not excited to sit around in my sister's shadow the whole time."

"That sucks," says Luke. "I'm sorry."

"She's pregnant, by the way." I press my lips together. *Focus, Emma. Focus.* "Anyway, I, um—I was thinking that the trip might be more pleasant if I brought along a plus one. That way I'd no longer be the pitifully perpetual single girl, you know?"

"Come on, Emma. You're not pitiful."

"No, I know. But it sure feels that way when I'm around my family." I take a breath. "Anyway, I know this is probably going to sound nuts, but...I was wondering if you would consider coming along as my boyfriend. My fake boyfriend, I mean."

Luke laughs. Or, to be more accurate, he bursts out laughing. Immediately, my stomach sinks.

Then Luke looks at me and his face drops. "Wait. You're serious?"

Should I pretend that I was joking? Is this a sinking ship that I should abandon? No. Come on. I can't give up this easily.

I look at him solemnly. "I'm serious."

"Wow," says Luke. "I...uh..."

"You'll get a free vacation out of it," I say. "My parents always insist on picking up the tab for the hotel and food and everything. And I have a bunch of extra miles, so I'd cover your airfare."

I cringe at the desperation coating each word that tumbles out of my mouth. Why did I think this would be a good idea? Why didn't I at least sleep on it, like a rational person? I study Luke's face, trying to gauge how he's feeling about my proposition now that he knows I'm not kidding around.

Unfortunately for me, his expression is one of indisputable pity.

"Look, Emma," he says. "I'm sympathetic to your

situation. I really am. But...sorry, it's kind of...I don't know. I don't know if I could do something like that."

I knew it. I *knew* it was a stupid idea. I lower my eyes. "It's okay. I understand."

"Besides, wouldn't it be easier to get a *real* boyfriend to show off to your family?"

I know that Luke is just trying to help. But the question stings anyway. The only person I'm interested in is Alex, and I've never gotten the slightest hint that he likes me back. Why oh why do I have to like someone so unattainable? It's like I'm trying to stay single on purpose.

I'm about to tell Luke to forget that I ever asked. Before I can, though, someone bumps into our table, knocking over my coffee. The coffee floods the tabletop, then spills over onto the floor. I thrust my chair out of the way.

"Oh, gosh," says the stranger, cupping her hand over her mouth. Her eyes go as wide as coffee lids. "I'm *so* sorry."

Luke is already out of his seat, grabbing practically the entire reserve of napkins from the condiment bar. Kneeling, he presses them to the floor. They soak through instantly.

He looks up at me. "Any get on you?"

I shake my head.

"Let me buy you a new coffee," the stranger says.

"Don't worry about it," I say.

"Are you sure?" the stranger says. "I'm so sorry, I didn't—"

"I'm *fine*," I snap. I stand up and grab my things. But of course the strap of my bag gets tangled on the back of the chair, and as I yank it off, I topple the chair in the process. I pull the chair upright, hook the freed strap over my shoulder, grab my empty cup, and toss it in the trash on my way out.

Outside of the café, Luke catches up with me. "Hey, are you okay? I really *am* sorry. I wish I could say yes."

"It was a dumb idea."

"It's not dumb. I just don't think I'm—"

"No, it's dumb," I say.

Luke and I head back to the office in uncomfortable silence. Like, an even-breathing-feels-too-loud uncomfortable silence.

As we walk into the building, my phone chimes. It's a text from Catherine, sent to the whole family. She's texted us a link to a vacation rental, along with the note, *Found the perfect place.*

I shove my phone back into my pocket. Luke hits the call button for the elevator, which lights up citrine yellow. For the longest minute of my life, we stand side by side in the empty lobby, still not speaking to each other.

"What if—" Luke starts to say, then stops himself.

I wait for him to continue.

"Never mind," he says.

2

AT LEAST WE don't get trapped in the elevator.

As soon as the elevator doors open to our floor, though, I mumble something about seeing him later and flee in the opposite direction, going down the hall to the bathrooms. In the privacy of a locked stall, I drop my head into my hands and let out a long sigh.

A few minutes later, when I emerge, I see that I'm no longer alone in the bathroom. Paige is standing at the sink brushing her teeth. As you do at work.

"Ehmmah," says Paige, her mouth full of suds. She spits into the sink and wipes her mouth with the back of her hand. "I had a dream about you last night."

"Oh?" I say, pumping candy-pink hand soap out of the dispenser.

"It was your wedding," says Paige, dreamily. "And oh my *gosh* was it beautiful."

Who knows? Maybe Paige is clairvoyant. But I

don't take the bait. I know better. Once you start asking Paige questions, it snowballs. It's best to just smile and nod.

"Are you doing anything tonight?" she asks. She grins at me—or, rather, her reflection in the mirror grins at me. There's a glob of toothpaste drying in the corner of her mouth.

"Um," I say. I don't want to tell her my actual plans, but I can't think of any other excuses fast enough. "Yeah. I'm going to Dance Den."

"Dance Den!" Paige's eyes light up like neon. "I've always been curious about that place. How often do you go?"

"Oh...now and then," I say.

Please don't invite yourself along. Please don't invite yourself along.

Paige plops her toothbrush into its semi-transparent carrying case and snaps it shut. She slides the case into her toiletry bag, then pulls out a travel hairbrush and begins to drag it through her wavy locks. As she does so, I put my hand on the bathroom door handle and pull it open. But before I can escape, Paige pipes up again.

"I'll have to check out the schedule," she says.

Damn it.

Well, at least she didn't invite herself along tonight.

I smile and nod. I exit the bathroom. On my way back to my desk, I make a pit stop in the break room to pour myself a cup of coffee—one that hopefully doesn't end up on the floor this time. But when I open up the cabinet above the sink to get my mug—my cat mug, which I always keep here at work—I don't see it anywhere. Nor is it in any other cabinet that I check.

Once more, to be sure, I hunt through the upper cabinet where people store the mugs they've brought from home. There are cheesy joke mugs, bulbous ceramic mugs, customized photo mugs. None, however, are mine. Mine has a picture of a tabby cat's sleepy face on it, and when filled with hot liquid, the tabby's face becomes alert and joyful. It's silly, and cute, and never ceases to entertain me.

But now, like a lost cat, it's missing.

Annoyed, I grab one of the plain communal mugs from another shelf, splash coffee into it, and head to my desk. I spend the next few hours working. But in the back of my head, I keep reliving the embarrassment I felt earlier in front of Luke, and every time I grab my coffee mug to take a sip out of it, the lack of cat face annoys me more and more.

I open up my chat application and click on Luke's name. *Someone stole my cat mug.*

It takes him a few minutes to write back. *What?*
My cat mug! I couldn't find it in the break room.
You really think someone stole it?
Yes.
Another few minutes pass. *That sucks.*
I know, I type. *It does suck.*

Several more minutes pass, and Luke doesn't type anything else. I drum my fingers on my desk, trying to think of how I can get things back to normal between us. Should I joke about making a LOST CAT sign for my mug? Should I come up with a list of suspects? I know what I *should* be doing—working—but I'm too distracted to get any real work done.

Eventually, I give up trying to say something witty and simply type, *Can we forget about earlier?*

Sure, responds Luke.

Cool. Thanks. I feel a weight lifted off my shoulders. *So anyway...*

Sorry, meeting, Luke types. *brb.*

But later, when he gets back to his desk, he doesn't type anything into our chat window. It remains idle for the rest of the day. And at the end of the day, after I pack up my stuff, I glance over at his desk and see that he's already gone.

So much for leaving work together like we normally do.

I know I'm probably turning this into a bigger deal than it is. But I can't help feeling like he's avoiding me now. I can't help feeling like I crossed a line I shouldn't have in our friendship. And now I have to pay the price.

* * *

I GO from work directly to Dance Den. Which is pretty much my favorite place in the whole world. What *is* Dance Den, you ask? Well, it's a place you dance. Obviously. And it's a place you work out. But it's so much more than that. And between the stress I'm feeling about the family vacation and the mess I've made with Luke, it's *exactly* what I need right now.

The parking lot is full, as usual, so I park a few blocks away. I grab my workout bag from my trunk and devour a pre-dance energy bar as I head over. As I walk up to the building, I already start feeling relaxed. And the moment I enter, it's like being transported into another world. A cathartic, nonjudgmental, soothing alternate world.

When I first heard about Dance Den, I assumed it was some kind of weird underground club or something. The idea of dancing barefoot in the basement of a community center with a bunch of strangers held exactly zero appeal to me.

But one day, after an especially annoying exchange with Catherine, I was online searching for ways to destress and an article about Dance Den popped up. And for whatever reason, it didn't sound so crazy anymore.

So I went.

And I loved it.

And I've been going ever since.

Tonight, when I walk in, there's already a good-sized number of people in attendance. People are using every available space to stretch. Some of them are keeping to themselves, some of them are chatting. I don't know any of their names, but by now they're almost all familiar faces, and that brings me a special kind of comfort.

I go up to the check-in desk and pay my ten dollars and write my name on the sign-in form. Then I step into the bathroom to peel out of my work clothes and get into my dance clothes: a sports bra, a light loose-fitting tee, and my favorite bright purple leggings. I get changed just in time. When I enter the studio, everyone's spreading out and finding their place.

Carla, the founder of Dance Den—a bright-eyed woman with lavender-dyed hair who teaches fitness classes to seniors when she's not here—welcomes everyone with an energetic greeting. Everyone in the room collectively returns her cheerful hello.

"Is everyone ready to dance?" Carla calls out.

"Yes!" we all shout back.

"Then let's get this dance party started!"

Tonight, as always, Carla starts us out with stretches. "Remember, folks, it's *so* important to warm up your body," she says. "I know you've been awake all day, but that doesn't mean your muscles are." She has us close our eyes, has us roll our heads forward and to the side and back and forward again, has us do shoulder rolls and hip circles and knee bends. There's no music playing as we warm up, just the sound of her voice interwoven with the sound of our collective breathing.

But after we finish warming up, the music quietly comes on. It's a gentle beat at first, nice and easy, and Carla encourages us to just *listen* and move our bodies as we please. It's the part of the evening I always feel the most awkward about—especially when it's crowded like it is tonight and we're all still figuring out how to dance without invading each other's personal space. But by the end of the song, any discomfort has worn off. I've gotten into a groove. I can feel it now in my bones. And as the music picks up, I follow along with it. I move. I sway my hips. I twirl. Along with the rest of my fellow dancers, I follow Carla's instructions as she shouts them above the music. We put our hands in the air. We jump. We dip. We spin.

It's always around the eighty-minute mark that something kind of magical happens. It's probably the main reason I keep coming back to Dance Den. In the minutes leading up to that point, I'm always so exhausted, so sweaty, so tired, that I don't know how I'm possibly going to survive the last twenty minutes. *I'm not going to make it this time*, I always think. *I'm going to have to bow out. I'm going to pass out if I keep going.* And yet I keep going. I push through, even though my sides are on fire. Even though the sweat is running into my eyes. And it's in those last handful of minutes that I feel totally unencumbered—that I feel simply, purely alive.

IT'S a little later that evening, when I'm on my way home, that I get the text from Luke. I have to read it multiple times to make sure I'm reading it right. After all, I *am* in an exhausted, half-delirious state, and I could easily be imagining the words I'm seeing on my phone.

But later, after I get home and shower, after I fix myself a proper dinner to eat, I look at my phone and the text from Luke is still there. The words haven't changed from when I read them earlier. He's up for it. The fake relationship. He's actually up for it.

Changed my mind, his text reads. *I'm in.*

3

A FEW HOURS after Luke tells me he's in, once it feels safe to say that he's not going to take it back, I text my family the news.

Hey guys, fyi, I invited my boyfriend to come on the trip too.

To my surprise, I'm actually nervous sending the text. I guess part of me is convinced that they'll see right through it, that my plan will fail before it even starts. I'm worried, too, that they won't be okay with me inviting someone along. It's unprecedented for me, after all.

I try to distract myself with cleaning out my fridge. But when I hear my phone chime, I drop what I'm doing. I mean, literally, I drop what I'm doing. A jar of salsa in my hand slips and accidentally crashes onto the floor.

Cursing, I tiptoe around the mess and run across the room to scoop up my phone.

Catherine has responded. *Boyfriend?*

His name is Luke, I text back. I unspool some paper towels and begin to clean up the mess of glass-spiked salsa that's now splattered across my kitchen floor like a crime scene.

A few minutes later, Mom chimes in. *Of course he's welcome to join us!*

I breathe out in relief. Then another text from Catherine pops up. *You're sharing a room, right? I've already booked our rental, and it only has four bedrooms.*

Yep, I text back. Right. Sleeping arrangements. I hadn't even thought about the fact that Luke and I would have to share a room. Well, whatever. He and I will figure that part out later.

Anything else we should know? asks Catherine.

What, like a city hall wedding that none of them were invited to? I laugh at the thought of proposing that to Luke. Now *that* would be something to fake.

Nope, I text.

Catherine doesn't send any more texts after that. But one does come through from Mom: *We look forward to meeting him, Emma.* And even though I know it's ridiculous, it pleases me as much as if this whole thing was the real deal.

THE FOLLOWING DAY, Luke and I go out to lunch to iron out the details. We go to Tasty Thai, of course. Tasty Thai is our go-to lunch spot—a restaurant we've frequented so often that as soon as the waitress seats us, she knowingly asks, "The regular?"

We smile and say yes. The regular is khao soi for Luke, chicken pad thai for me, and an order of spring rolls to share. And when I say spring rolls, I don't mean just any old spring rolls. The ones at Tasty Thai are little pieces of heaven. They're perfectly crisp, hot, and bewilderingly flavorful. If it was socially acceptable to eat nothing but a huge platter of their spring rolls for lunch, I would.

"So," says Luke, after the waitress leaves. "You're probably wondering what made me change my mind."

I pull my napkin out from beneath my cutlery and smooth it over my lap. "You would be correct."

"If I tell you, you've gotta promise you won't make fun of me."

"Intriguing. I don't know if I can promise that, though."

He blows air out between his lips. "Fine. Okay. You know Erin?"

"Erin from Accounting?"

"Yes. Erin from Accounting."

"Uh huh. What about her?"

"I kind of—" His eyes drift away from mine. "I have a thing for her. But she has the wrong impression of me. So I—"

"Whoa, whoa," I say, "You have a thing for her?"

Erin from Accounting is pretty. I'll give you that. She has that whole blonde-hair-nice-body thing going for her. Yet for some reason, I can't wrap my head around Luke having a thing for her. They just don't mesh. I can't imagine the two of them as a couple.

"You said you wouldn't make fun of me," says Luke.

"I'm not making fun of you," I say. "But as your friend, I have to say, I think she's all wrong for you."

"Great. Thanks."

"Sorry," I say. "Wait, what do you mean, she has the wrong impression of you?"

Luke sighs. "She thinks I'm a player."

"Um, what?" Is there a side to Luke that I'm unaware of? "Elaborate, please."

"It's just because of some stupid thing that Alex said. He was joking around about me being on this dating app all the time, and she thought he was serious."

The mention of Alex's name makes my ears perk up. I can't help but wonder if Alex is also on the dating app that he and Luke were talking about.

I start to ask, "What's the name of the—" But then the waitress appears beside our table and lowers the plate of appetizer perfection in front of us.

"Enjoy!" she says cheerfully.

We both thank her. At the sight—and smell—of the spring rolls, my salivary glands immediately kick into overdrive. But I need to focus. I'm still in a haze about what Luke is trying to tell me.

"Sorry, can we back up a second?" I say. "How is going on a vacation with *me* going to help you out with *Erin*?"

"I was getting to that," says Luke. "You interrupted me."

"I had critical questions," I say.

Okay. That's it. I can't hold back from the spring rolls any longer. I reach out and pluck one from the plate. I eagerly bring it to my mouth and sink my teeth in, eliciting that oh-so-satisfying crunch.

"So my whole point," continues Luke, "which I was about to get to, is that I need to prove to her that I am more than capable of commitment. That I'm not just some drooling skirt-chaser. So here's the deal. I'll be your fake boyfriend during your family vacation, but only if you be my fake girlfriend for the next three weeks at work."

Reflexively, I swallow the unchewed bite of spring roll in my mouth. The piece lodges in my throat. I swallow again, hard, painfully forcing it down.

"Um, what?" I rasp.

"We'd only have to fake it during office hours," he says. "I mean, come on. What's another few extra weeks?"

"But we'd have to lie to everyone."

Luke gives me a funny look. "Uh, with your plan, aren't people going to suspect something anyway? Don't you think us both taking a week-long vacation at the exact same time, to the exact same place, is going to raise some eyebrows?"

How did I not think of that? He's right, of course. Even if one of us lies about where we're going, our identical days off will definitely be a tip-off.

The waitress approaches the table, a steaming plate of food in each hand. She grins at me as she lowers my pad thai down in front of me. I wish I could ask for her opinion.

Her eyebrows lift questioningly. "Can I get you anything else?"

"Oh. No. We're good," I quickly say. "Thank you."

"Actually," says Luke, "could we get a spice rack?"

"That's right," the waitress says, grinning. "You like a bit of spice." She zips away and then comes back again, setting the little set of glass jars on our table with an amused smile. Has she been listening in on our conversation?

The waitress leaves, and I'm left to face the unanswered question.

"I dunno," I say. "I'm not crazy about the idea of turning this into an office romance. It's one thing to lie to my family...I only see them a couple times a year. But we're in the office every day."

"We won't have to do much."

"You really think it will convince Erin?"

Luke shrugs. "Maybe it won't. But it's worth a shot."

I really don't want to have to put up a facade for longer than necessary. And I really don't think that Erin is right for Luke. But...oh, what the hell. If that's what Luke wants out of it, I'll help him out. He's my friend. Anyway, it's not like I exactly have a choice at this point—I've already told my family about him.

"Fine," I say. "I'll do it."

Luke smiles. "Yeah? Cool."

"We're going to need a story, you know."

"A story?" Luke asks. He spoons a small amount of spice over his khao soi and mixes it in.

"About how this came about. Our...reciprocal attraction."

"Well, first off, let's maybe not use the phrase 'reciprocal attraction.' Because that's definitely not going to convince anyone."

"You know what I mean."

Luke takes a bite of his lunch and studies me thoughtfully as he chews. Feeling suddenly self-conscious, I grab another spring roll. I bite, chew, swallow. But of course that only makes me feel more self-conscious. No one likes to be watched while they eat.

Luke swallows and snaps his fingers. "I know," he says, wiping off a near-invisible smear of sauce from the side of his mouth. "It happened during the team building exercise. Our eyes met from opposite sides of the spaghetti tower, and the rest was history."

That is eerily too close to how I came up with this idea in the first place. I can't explain why, but I can't have that be our story. "No. That's just...no."

"Got any other suggestions?"

"Not yet. I'll think of something." I clear my throat. "We also need to set some ground rules. Like...no going on actual dates with other people, obviously."

"That's fine."

"And no PDA."

"Of course not," he says, screwing up his face in a way that I would be offended by if I wasn't making the same face myself.

"We'll have to fake a breakup, too. Once the vacation's over."

"What if we break up *during* the vacation? I mean, obviously, we wouldn't tell your family that, but..."

"...it could be the story we tell people at work," I say. I squeeze a wedge of lime over my pad thai. "Let's see. Maybe I could catch you oogling the hula dancers?"

"Googling the hula dancers? What?"

"Oogling," I repeat, slightly louder.

Luke bites back a laugh. "It's *ogle*. Not *oogle*."

"What?"

"Have you really been saying *oogle* your whole life instead of *ogle*?" It's clearly taking him an immense amount of willpower to not burst out laughing at me.

I exhale. "Can we focus, please?"

"Sorry." He shakes his head. "Anyway, I'd prefer if we didn't break up over me '*oogling*' other women. I'm trying to show Erin that I can commit to a relationship, remember?"

"Yeah, yeah," I say.

By the time we're done eating, we've figured it all out. Our story, if asked, is that we fell for each other one night over drinks (not *too* many drinks, I clarify; we don't want people thinking we were drunk), and at the end of the Hawaii trip, we'll split amicably, simply deciding that we're better off as friends. It's a boring breakup story, but one that will easily allow us to go back to being friends. We've also agreed that we'll come up with dates each week—not dates that we'll actually go on, but outings that we'll be able to reference around others if need be.

"Sounds like we're all set, then," says Luke.

I nod. "Well—actually, there is one other little thing."

He raises his eyebrows. He waits for me to continue.

"Would you...be open to telling my family that you own your own business?"

"Uh, why?"

I try to make it sound like it's no big deal. "It would impress my parents."

"Right," says Luke. He looks a little tired, but I'm hoping it's just from the Thai food. "Okay. Whatever. That's fine."

I let out a breath. "Thanks, Luke."

We don't say much to each other as we walk back to work. As we're riding the elevator up to our floor, though, Luke glances over at me and says, "So, we're starting now, right?"

"Uh, sure," I say, as the elevator slows to a stop. "I guess so."

And with that, we walk back into work together, officially in a fake relationship.

It feels as if it should be obvious that something is different with Luke and I when we arrive back in the office. But of course nobody can tell that anything's changed. On the surface, we appear exactly as we did when we left, just as the office looks and sounds and smells like the same old office as ever. Same old whirr of the copy machine, same old trill of the phones, same old looks on our coworkers' faces in the maze of cubicles.

There *is* something going on over by Luke's desk, though. A small group of people have gathered by the window over there. After exchanging glances, Luke and I walk over and join them. From the edge of the gathered group, I rise up on my tiptoes to see what they're all so captivated by. And what I see is the last thing I would expect: down on the sidewalk, a crow and a squirrel are in some kind of standoff.

The squirrel darts toward the crow. The crow gives a warning flap of its wings and the squirrel backs off again. Half the people around us cheer. I scan the crowd for Erin from Accounting's face—I keep thinking about how nuts it is that Luke likes her—but she's nowhere in sight.

"Oh, come *on*, squirrel!" someone says. "Don't back down!"

"He's gonna lose," someone else says.

"Five bucks says he won't," says a third.

It goes on like that—the standoff, the cheering—for another full five minutes. Then someone notices Sherrie coming and the group scatters like buckshot. Back at my cubicle, I open my desk's wonky upper drawer, fish out a mint from the pack I keep there, and then I get back to usual grind: sorting through the non-stop queue of vendor applications that have come in from potential artisans.

When I first started this job, the idea that I was going to get to decide who got through to the senior inventory buyers and who didn't was definitely an ego boost. I had so much power! I could tell people no! Or yes! (Well, not yes, exactly, but I could pass them on up the chain.) But when I actually started doing it, it quickly became apparent how unglamorous the task is. The majority of the artisans who apply can be put into the *no* pile within a matter of seconds, either because of their far-too-homemade-looking wares, their poorly filled out application, or, in the majority of cases, both.

I am, essentially, a human spam filter.

I open up the folder on the server where all the applications get funneled. And for the next few hours, that's where I stay. Of the forty-seven applications I review, only five are decent enough to forward on to the senior buyers. One is so bad that I can't *not* email it to Luke. The applicant in question is a maker of handsewn hemp underwear—and under the *Location* section of her application has written MOTHER EARTH.

From my chair, if I sit up perfectly straight, I can see the back of Luke's head and some of his desk. And I can see his monitor *just* well enough to see him immediately open the link I've sent him and take in the glory that is this woman's portfolio.

A few seconds later, an instant message from Luke pops up on my screen. *So you're saying you want a bunch of these undies for Christmas?*

Very funny, I type back.

Looks like she'll even sew your name in them...

Don't do it. Don't you dare.

I force myself to go back to the applications. If I don't keep up with them, the backlog will quickly become unbearable. But I can only get through another half dozen before switching back over to the chat conversation with Luke.

So, I type. *What's the new couple up to this weekend?*

Hmm...movie? he types back.

Sure.

Let's see that new superhero one. Saturday night?

It's a date.

A few minutes pass, and then a new message from Luke pops up. *There's an 8pm showing. Pick you up at 7:30?*

My fingers hover over the keyboard. Wait, we're not making *real* plans, are we? I assumed we were just coming up with our shared alibi. I glance over at Luke—at the back of his head, that is—but of course that doesn't help me out at all.

I feel dumb typing what I type next. But I need to make sure we're on the same page. *Um...we're not actually going, right?*

He replies, *Correct...*

My feeling of dumbness doubles. *Okay. That's what I thought. I was just checking. Sorry.*

Right, Luke replies.

THAT WEEKEND, I do all my normal weekend things: sleep in, cook myself a decent breakfast, read, soak in the tub, deep clean my apartment. I don't think about the movie date that Luke and I supposedly have gone on until late Sunday evening, when I realize that I should probably read a review or something so that if it *does* come up in conversation, it's not totally obvious that I haven't seen it.

"I mean, I thought the visual effects were *amazing*," I practice aloud, after reading up on the superhero movie. "But talk about plot holes, am I right?"

I couldn't sound less convincing if I tried.

That night, I doze off in the middle of reading more reviews. In the morning, I wake up from a dream that I was *in* the movie. Not as in acting in it, but as in existing in that world. I am relieved, to say the least, that this is not actually the case.

I get up, I get ready for the day, I get myself to the office. As usual, I head to the break room to pour myself a cup of coffee—using another communal mug, since, much to my disgruntlement, my cat cup still hasn't turned up. I'm stirring in the sugar when footsteps enter the break room and Lucinda's voice greets me. Lucinda works with the marketing team. She's also the office gossip.

"Morning, Emma!" she sings.

"Hi, Lucinda."

"Have a nice weekend?"

I nod. "I did. And you?"

"Oh, it was *wonderful*. It was so beautiful out, wasn't it? I love this time of year." Then, slightly lowering her voice, she says, "So, you and Luke, huh? That's so exciting, Emma."

I clank my spoon against the cup. "Come again?"

"I heard about you two love birds," she says. She gives me a knowing grin. "I think it's really sweet."

I smile nervously. "Who did you hear that from?"

"Luke, silly," she says. "I rode the elevator up with him this morning, and he told me about your date this weekend."

"Ah," I say. Well, at least it came from the source. "Right. Yeah, the movie, it, um—it was great. The acting...and the plot..."

"Wait! Don't ruin it for me," says Lucinda. "I'm going to see it next weekend. I can't *wait*. Oh! Emma. I just had a thought. You and Luke should come bowling with Beau and I tomorrow night. We're going to Balmer Lanes."

"Um, sorry?"

"Bowling," she says. "You know." She pantomimes throwing a bowling ball down a lane, as if I've never encountered the activity before. "Now that you and Luke are an item, we can go on a double date together."

"Oh," I say. The word comes out of my mouth far too high-pitched. "Well, I'll have to check with Luke."

"Please do," says Lucinda. "Let me know as soon as you talk to him, okay? I *really* hope you two can make it."

I force my mouth into a smile and nod. Then I grab my coffee and leave the break room. As I walk to my desk, I swear that I can feel the news about Luke and I spreading through the office.

My desk feels like it's miles away. Finally, having reached it, I drop down in my chair and open my ongoing instant message conversation with Luke.

You told Lucinda?

Luke's reply comes swiftly. *How else were people going to find out?*

I guess he has a point. It's not like we can sashay around the office holding hands. Telling the office gossip will easily take care of spreading the word.

Fine, whatever, I type. *But FYI, we've been invited to go bowling with Lucinda and her husband. Any great ideas for excuses?*

There's a pause before Luke replies. *Why do we have to give an excuse?*

You actually want to go?

It's not about wanting to go. It's about doing things that couples do.

I quietly grumble to myself. *I thought we didn't have to go on any real dates.*

Don't think of it as a date, then. We're just hanging out.

Well, that wasn't the reaction I was expecting from Luke. But fine. If he thinks it's a good idea to go, we'll go.

Okay, I type. *I'll tell her yes.*

4

LUKE PICKS me up outside my apartment just after seven on Tuesday night. It's weird seeing him outside of work. It's because of the clothes, I think. I've gotten so used to his long-sleeved collared shirts and business casual chinos that seeing him in anything else delivers a little shock to my system.

He's dressed in jeans and a short sleeve tee that leaves his arms all...exposed. It's strange that I've worked with Luke for six years and never actually seen his arms, right?

No, actually, what's strange is that I'm thinking about his arms in the first place.

I shift around uselessly in the passenger seat, but I'm uncomfortable no matter how I position myself.

"Everything okay over there?" Luke asks, not taking his eyes off the road.

"Uh huh," I cough out. "Peachy keen."

I snap down the sun visor and check what little makeup I've put on. It's all still there. I squint at my reflection, commanding myself to have no more mystifying thoughts about Luke. But then I catch a flash of stripes in the mirror, and I realize something that makes my chest constrict.

I'm wearing a shirt that is identical to Luke's.

My eyes dart over to confirm it. Oh, no. It's not just our shirts. It's our jeans, too. They look like they've been cut from the same bolt of distressed indigo wash denim. Even the *stitching* is identical.

"Turn the car around," I say, squeezing my hands into fists to stop them from grabbing the steering wheel. "I need to go home and change."

Luke shoots me a split-second glance. "What?"

"We're twins, Luke. We can't show up like this."

"Twins?" he says. Then he looks over again, sees what I mean, and laughs. "At least everyone there will know we're together."

"Please turn the car around."

"Sorry. No can do. We're already late as it is."

"Luke!"

"Relax. Nobody is going to care."

"*I* care. I don't want to be one of those weird matchy-matchy couples." I desperately swivel to survey his back seat. There's a gym bag, some windshield flyers, a stray phone charger. But not a single spare shirt. "Tell me you have one of your work button-ups in your trunk."

Luke snorts. "You really don't want to go bowling, do you?"

"It's not—I just don't—" I huff out a breath. I hate that we're dressed like this. I hate looking like an idiot. But, apparently, it's out of my control. Luke's not turning this car around. I'm just going to have to grit my teeth and bear it.

Ten minutes later, we're circling the packed-full parking lot of Balmer Lanes like a vulture waiting for its prey to croak. Finally, Luke sees a car backing out and careens into the spot as soon as the sedan pulls away. There's barely any space for me to open my door and squeeze out of the car, and I'm about to be annoyed at Luke, until I look over and see him having to squeeze out of his side of the car, too.

Then, side by side, in our stupid matching outfits, we head into the aging one-story building. We're immediately enveloped in the noise as we open the front doors. It's busy in here tonight, packed in as if lives depend on it. The woody crash of pins falling punctuates the air. It smells like wood and grease and sweat and nerves.

Among the crowd, I see a hand waving, a flash of bright auburn hair coming over to greet us.

"Hey, you two!" Lucinda calls out as she approaches. "Aw, cute. You color coordinated!"

I shoot a look at Luke.

"Hi, Lucinda," he says, ignoring my glare. "Wow. It's busy in here tonight."

Lucinda's voice goes up half an octave. "Right? We lucked out and got the last lane of the night. Oh, and by the way, I invited—"

As Lucinda talks, it's as if the volume of the alley suddenly turns down, and I hear with perfect clarity a familiar laugh. I lean slightly to the left and see none other than Paige.

Lucinda is saying, "—figured the more the merrier, you know? Have you two ever met Paige's boyfriend?"

I'm too busy trying to think of an escape plan to answer.

Beside me, Luke says, "Nope. We haven't."

"Well, he's great," says Lucinda. "You'll love him."

In lane eight, we're greeted by Paige's toothy smile. She's doing warm-up stretches, bending one arm over her head at a time.

"There you are! Did you get lost?" says Paige as she rolls her head from shoulder to shoulder.

An obscenely muscular guy hunched over the lane's touchscreen turns his whole body in the seat and says, "You must be Emmaline and Luke. Hi. I'm Martin."

"It's just Emma," I say, extending a hand. His meaty paw envelops mine.

"And this is Beau," says Lucinda. I turn and shake her husband's hand. Beau is pretty much exactly what I expect. Picture as regular of a guy in his mid-thirties as you can imagine, and that's Beau.

"It's nice to meet you two," says Beau. "Lucinda said you all work together, right?"

I nod at Beau. I want to be friendly, I want to say something more, but I don't really know what to add. I can't exactly say, *Yeah, I don't want to be here right now, Luke and I aren't even actually together,* now can I?

"You really should do some stretches, Emma," says Paige. "Here. Come join me."

"Um, that's okay," I say, and look over at Luke with *help me* eyes.

"You know what," says Luke, snapping his fingers, "I'm going to grab us shoes."

"I'll go with you," I say quickly.

"No need," says Luke. "Just tell me what size you wear."

I know it's silly to be embarrassed about saying my shoe size. It's not like people can't see my feet. But it's always been something I've been sensitive about. Whenever I have to say my shoe size aloud, I get a flashback of my friends in fourth grade laughing their heads off.

"Nine and a half," I mumble. "But sometimes I'm a ten. Which is why I should go with you. To try on both sizes."

"They don't have half sizes," says Paige, loudly, as she bends over to touch her tiny, unfairly dainty feet. "You have to size up."

Luke disappears to get our shoes. Paige transitions into stretching out her hamstrings. Martin busies himself with fixing my name up on the screen.

"So," I say. "Um, how long have you two been together?"

"Me and Martin?" says Paige. "Oh, we go *way* back."

"Way back," says Martin, giving Paige a suggestive smile.

"Ah," I say.

Martin leans back in his chair. "How about The High Rollers?"

"Sorry?" I say.

"For our team name."

"I think it would be fun if we combined all of our initials," says Paige. "Does that spell anything?"

"Sorry, babe. I don't think that will work," says Martin. "Emma? Any suggestions?"

"Not yet," I say.

While they continue to debate potential team names, I excuse myself to pick out a bowling ball. Over at the rack, I dawdle, testing out ball after ball. I run my hands over them, picking one up and then another, giving each a ridiculous amount of consideration. When Luke walks past with our shoes, I call him over.

"Want to make a run for it?" I ask.

He frowns at me. "I just got our shoes. By the way, they didn't have your size. I had to get you a men's size eight instead."

"Are you kidding me?" I say. "Okay. We need to go. Let's say that I'm coming down with something."

"They're just shoes, Emma."

"It's not just that. It's…" I glance over my shoulder at Paige. "It's *her*."

"Come on. It won't be that bad."

I grumble. "Famous last words."

"You're saying that bowling with Paige is going to kill you? A tad dramatic, don't you think?"

I grab the disinfectant-reeking bowling shoes from his hands. "Fine. Give me those."

We rejoin the group just in time to see Paige pull a bowling ball out of her own personal carrying case. Of *course* she would have her own bowling ball. As she runs a cloth over the high-gloss surface, the polish catches a ray of light and glares in my eyes.

Martin stands up from the console, all eight million feet of him unfolding.

"All right," he says, lifting a massive ball from the return. "Wish me luck."

As Martin bowls and gets a spare, a feeling of dread starts to creep into my stomach. Paige goes next, knocking down eight out of the ten pins. Then Lucinda goes, then Beau, who each knock down a decent amount, too. By the time it's Luke's turn, I actually do start to feel sick.

Am I really the only one in the group who's bad at this?

"I can't believe how good those kids are," says Lucinda, and I snap out of my misery for a few seconds to follow her gaze over to the lane next to us, which is filled with what looks like a bunch of seven-year-olds. Right after she says it, one of them throws a spare.

"Wow, yeah," I say.

"They're so adorable," says Lucinda.

One of the kids emits an earsplitting scream. I wince and touch my ear. I turn and watch as Luke knocks down one of his remaining three pins, shakes his head, and then nods at me. "You're up, Armstrong. Show us what you've got."

When I say I'm bad at bowling, I'm not exaggerating. Actually, scratch that. I am *awful*. There's just something about bowling that brings out all the awkwardness and inability in me.

Reluctantly, I approach the ball return. I eye the little lemon yellow ball that I selected from the rack. Maybe this time will be different. Things can inexplicably change, right?

I slide my fingers into its holes, pick it up. It feels like it's the exact right weight. Okay. I've got this. We can do this, little lemon yellow bowling ball. I'll do my part and release you; you just have to knock down the pins. Deal?

I approach the lane. My feet slide in my ill-fitting shoes. I try to channel the bowlers who have worn the shoes before me—surely there had to be one master among them.

I bring the ball to my chest. Then I take three little steps, swinging the ball back, and—just before my toe goes over the foul line—I heave my arm forward and send the ball down the lane. It lands with a thud on the floor, then goes spinning toward its destination.

And then it veers. And veers. And into the gutter it goes.

"Tough luck," says Martin.

"You should've stretched," Paige says, cracking her neck.

"It happens to all of us," Lucinda says.

I turn and slump down into my seat. In the next lane over, the kids can't stop giggling.

FIVE FRAMES LATER—AFTER four more frames that make it seem like I'm trying to miss the bowling pins on purpose—Luke finally offers to help. Apparently five frames is the maximum number that he can take watching me make an utter fool of myself.

I pick up my traitorous lemon yellow ball and take my stance at the end of the lane. Luke, standing beside me now, shakes his head and tells me to hold the ball to my side.

"What do you mean? Like this?"

"No. More like this." He reaches out and moves my arms into what is apparently the correct position. "Then, when you swing your arm back, it'll go in a straight line, instead of a curve around your body."

"Gotcha."

"Now, when you drop your arm back down," he says, "remember that you're letting gravity do the work.

You're not throwing the ball. You're releasing it. Think of your arm as a ramp."

Everything Luke is saying makes perfect sense. It's so obvious, actually. Why has no one ever taught me this before?

"Show me your swing," he says.

I pull my arm back.

"You're still curving. Your arm should go back more like this." This time, Luke guides my arm up into the arc, his hands gently but firmly guiding my own. I can't help but tense up. It's weird, him being so close to me like this. And it's *really* weird, his hands on mine. His bicep is almost touching me. Who knew that Luke had muscles?

"God, you're tense," he says. "Try to loosen up. It'll help. Now keep your eye on one of the arrows on the lane. Aim for that, not the pins."

"I've got it," I say, yanking my arm out of his grasp. "Thanks."

Luke steps away, and I center myself. I keep the ball to my side. I pick out an arrow on the lane, take a few steps forward as I draw back the ball, then swing my arm forward and let the ball roll out of my hand.

The ball rolls. It goes straight down the lane. It's not going that fast, but it's going straight. And as we all watch, it keeps going. And going. And then I...I roll a...*strike*.

Paige tackles me with a hug. "Emma! You

superstar!" she shouts. I'm so stunned that I don't even care that she's practically strangling me.

After Paige lets go, Martin gives me a high five—a high five that leaves my palm stinging. Lucinda and Beau give me hearty congratulations right after.

I look at Luke. "Thanks, dude," I say.

"It was all you," he says.

"Your gutterball girlfriend just got a *strike*, Luke!" says Paige. "Jeez. Give her a kiss or something!"

I see Luke's face freeze. Mine freezes, too. *No*, I tell him with my eyes. *You are not allowed to kiss me.* But we can't just brush it off, either. Paige, freakin' Paige, she's standing there with her hands over her heart, waiting for us to embrace.

Luke laughs. Awkwardly. He steps toward me and wraps his arms around me, giving me a squeeze as he says, "Good job, um, babe."

"Thanks," I say. I am so uncomfortable, our bodies pressed together like this. I am so uncomfortable, I want to die.

Luke finally lets go. Thank God. I stare down at my shoes, sure that my face is bright red.

"Break for snacks?" Luke suggests.

"Yes," I say quickly. "Snacks sound good."

THE SIX OF us crowd into a big, slightly sticky booth in the dining area up above the lanes. We've ordered a bunch of stuff and put it all into the middle of the table like a smorgasbord: fish and chips, nachos, chicken tenders, and beers all around. For crappy bowling alley food, it's actually not that bad.

"This is fun, right?" says Lucinda. "It's really nice being able to hang out like this outside of the office." Then she grins at Luke and me and says, "Also, I just have to say. I'm so glad you two are together now. I always thought you would make a cute couple."

My stomach flips over. "You did, huh?" I say.

"Oh, definitely," says Lucinda. "I'm not alone in feeling that way, either."

Seriously? People at work think Luke and I should be together? Did Lucinda take a survey or something? Is this a frequent topic of conversation?

"If you two get married," says Paige, "you should have the wedding at the office. Wouldn't that be funny?"

"Why would they want to have a funny wedding, Paige?" says Lucinda.

"Well, they should at least incorporate work somehow," says Paige.

Oh, God. Next thing I know, she's going to ask to be a bridesmaid.

Furtively, I glance over at Luke. Unsurprisingly, he's keeping it cool. He simply continues to munch on the communal french fries like everyone is talking about the weather.

But everyone's not talking about the weather. They're talking about our hypothetical wedding.

"When my cousin got married," says Paige, "they had a live bagpiper play. It. Was. *Amazing*."

"We could probably get you the guy's info if you want," says Martin.

Really? He's in on this, too?

Lucinda squints at my hair and says how pretty it would look up in curls.

"Do you ever wear it like that, Emma?" she asks.

I shake my head and shove a fry into my mouth. I desperately try to think of a way to change the subject. Should I say something about bowling? About the food? Maybe I should upturn the table? I size up the table. Would I even be strong enough to do that?

Then, suddenly, I know what to say. Of *course*. Why didn't I think of it sooner?

"Lucinda," I say, sitting up straighter in my seat, "Not to change the subject, but have you heard any good gossip lately?"

Lucinda's eyes drop from my hair. They take on a twinkle.

I knew she couldn't resist.

"Actually, yes," she says, and her voice lowers into a hush. "I heard that Sherrie is going to be leaving soon. And you know what that means."

"Going away party?" asks Paige, then double-dips a fry.

Lucinda shoots her a look. "It means they're going to need someone to step into her spot."

"She's been there a long time, hasn't she?" asks Beau.

"Over a decade," says Lucinda, leaning back in her seat. "You should apply for the position, Emma."

I almost laugh. Me? As a supervisor? No. No way. I wouldn't be any good at managing people.

"If anyone's well-suited for it, that would be Luke," I say.

Luke chews thoughtfully on a nacho chip. "Yeah," says Luke. "I would apply."

I experience a momentary flash of what it would be like if Luke was our manager. Forget about feeling weird about seeing Luke's muscular arms. Luke being my manager would be *weird*.

"Last fry," announces Lucinda, pushing the little paper boat across the table toward us.

"Go for it, Armstrong," Luke says.

"AREN'T you glad we stuck it out?" asks Luke. We're back in his car, headed home. It's dark out now and the city feels different in that way that nighttime changes places. Crazily enough, I'm actually a little sad that bowling date night is over. As much as I wasn't looking forward to the night, I did end up having fun. I didn't throw any more strikes, but I didn't throw any more gutter balls, either—a win in my book.

"Can you believe that's Paige's boyfriend?" I say.

Luke laughs. "No. Never in a million years."

"And when Lucinda said that thing about always having imagined us together?"

"Yeah."

A second-too-long of silence passes between us.

"Anyway," I say. "Next time you go out on a date, you should totally take the girl bowling."

"Why's that?"

"Come on! You have skills!" I drum my fingers on my thighs. "And that 'correct your form' stuff is the perfect excuse to get all cozy."

He gives me a strange look. "I was trying to help you."

"Oh, I know." I clear my throat. "Do you think Sherrie is really leaving?"

"Who knows," he says. "If she did, though, you really wouldn't apply?"

I shrug. "I don't think I'd be good at it."

"I think you would."

"Well, thanks. But I still think you would be better."

"Okay," Luke says. "How about this? We'll talk them into giving us *both* the job. We'll be co-managers."

"Now that I could get behind." I point out at the road. "Take a turn at the light."

"Seriously, though...don't you have any higher aspirations?"

"What, like being the CEO of my own gifting business? I can see it now: *Emma's Exotic Imports*."

"You know what I mean." Luke lets his fingers slide

down the steering wheel. I glance at his arms. I momentarily think about them guiding mine, then shove the thought away. Luke asks, "When you were a kid, what did you say you wanted to be when you grew up?"

I don't answer right away. I look out the window, watch the passing houses. I'm trying to decide whether to tell the truth or offer up a white lie.

Luke glances over at me. "Well? Doctor? Ballerina? Mathematician?"

"A dog," I say.

"Um, what?"

I sigh. "When I was little, and someone asked me that question, I'd tell them I wanted to be a dog. I think it's because our neighbors had this great big Bernese Mountain Dog that I was obsessed with."

Silence fills the car. Several seconds of it pass. Then it's pierced by Luke's hearty laughter. And I start laughing along with him. Why I considered saying anything else beats me.

When my eyes dry, we've reached the block my apartment building is on.

"Thanks for driving," I say.

"No problem," he says. "It's what boyfriends do, right? Besides, now you owe me one."

I scoff. "Excuse me? You offered to drive. You practically insisted."

"Doesn't mean you don't owe me one."

"Right," I say, and roll my eyes. "Goodnight." But as

I unbuckle my seat belt, there is also this weird little twinge of sadness that unexpectedly surges through me. Because I can't help think about how if I did actually have a boyfriend, this is the kind of stuff that we would do. This is the way that I would come home at night, instead of already being in bed at this hour.

Well, whatever. It is what it is.

I get out of the car and start to walk away. Then I hear Luke call my name through the open window.

I turn around. "Yeah?"

"Let's try not to dress alike tomorrow, huh?" he says.

I smile. "I call dibs on blue."

5

EVERYTHING FEELS SLIGHTLY different at work the next day, although I can't quite explain how. I guess it feels as if Luke and I have passed some kind of initiation ritual and can be accepted around the office as a couple now. It especially feels like I'm a new member of a club when I walk by Lucinda's desk and hear her telling our coworkers about what a blast we all had at Balmer Lanes.

Then I notice that one of the people listening to Lucinda is Erin from Accounting, and I'm reminded that this whole thing is temporary and fake. I guess it's good, though, that Erin is there to hear about yesterday evening. It's exactly what Luke would want. I still don't think Erin is right for Luke, but if that's who he likes, that's who he likes.

When it doesn't work out between the two of them, though, I'm *so* telling him that I told him so.

I'm in the break room later that day when Paige comes in. She opens up the fridge, pulls out a carton of creamer with a note on it that reads DO NOT USE, and tips it into her coffee. Mid-pour, she glances up at me and smiles.

"Did you try the bread yet?" she asks.

"What?" I say.

"The bread," she says, nodding toward the counter. There's a foil-wrapped loaf there that I hadn't seen. As soon as I notice it, though, I immediately know that it's one of Paige's creations.

"It's ham and banana," she says.

"You know," I say. "I think I'll grab a slice later."

"It might be all gone by then. Take a piece now!"

Carefully, I peel back the foil. The bread looks very...moist.

"Wait," says Paige. "Here's a knife."

I cut off the thinnest piece possible, which is difficult, considering the chunks of ham strewn throughout the loaf. Paige grins at me eagerly, waiting for me to take a bite. And so I do. It's...meaty. And fruity. And disconcertingly crunchy.

I can't chew it any longer. I swallow the glob of meaty-fruity-bread.

"I've never had anything like it," I say.

Paige waits.

"It's good," I force out.

"Thanks," says Paige, flashing me a grin. She takes a sip of her coffee. "So, that was fun last night, huh?"

"It was."

"We should hang out again sometime."

Crap. I *knew* it was a bad idea to go bowling.

Before I can reply, though, Paige says, "Are you free this Friday? There's this new fusion place that Martin and I have been dying to go to. It's French-Asian, I think? Or, wait. Maybe Mexican-Asian. I'll need to look it up again. It's *something* Asian. Do you like Japanese food, Emma?"

"Oh, you know, we actually can't on Friday," I say. I inch closer to the door. "Sorry."

"Maybe next week, then?" she says. "What's your schedule look like?"

"Next week's pretty busy, too," I say.

Paige seems completely unfazed by my excuses. "Well, let me know," she says, and then cuts herself a slice of the ham-and-banana bread.

I've just gotten back to my desk when my phone lights up with missed group texts from Catherine. Evidently, she has decided that we should get family photos taken while we're in Hawaii, and has already researched local photographers.

There are so many options, Catherine texts. *But here's my faves. Thoughts?*

I click the first link that she's sent and it brings up a website brimming with photos taken at sunset; it's almost like no other time of day exists. The second link that I click opens up a much more streamlined website, with photos that are just as flawless.

By contrast, the last website is, to put it mildly, outdated. I half expect there to be a hit counter at the bottom of the page. But I like that the photographer's portfolio fells more genuine, less showy. He seems especially good at capturing candid shots.

I'm about to reply when Sherrie comes up to my desk and drums her fingers on the ledge of the cubicle. I quickly switch off the screen of my phone and place it face down and out of the way.

"Do you have a second, Emma?" Sherrie asks.

"Of course," I say. I smile, but inside, I'm kicking myself for not waking up my computer the moment I sat down. It looks like I'm just sitting here doing diddly-squat at my desk.

"I was taking a peek in the folder of rejected vendor applications earlier today," says Sherrie. "And I noticed a few missed gems in there."

"You did? Which ones?" I ask. Memories of badly knitted scarves and custom pet urns flash through my mind.

"Oh, you don't have to worry about that. I've already forwarded them to the senior buyers."

"Right, but if I knew which applications you thought had promise, I could—"

"I just want to make sure that you're giving each application a fair shake. That's all, Emma. Don't dismiss anything too quickly. Understood?"

"Understood."

Sherrie taps my cubicle again and starts to walk

away. But she makes it only a few steps before she turns and comes back.

"Oh," she says, and clicks her tongue against the roof of her mouth. "Also. I noticed that the backlog is getting pretty big. Don't let it get out of hand, okay?"

I give her a tight smile. It's all I can do not to sigh. So she wants me to take more time with each application, but also get through more of them, huh?

"Got it," I say.

After Sherrie leaves, I use one hand to tap my keyboard and wake up my computer and the other hand to flip my cell phone back over and quickly reply to the family group text. There's a bunch of missed texts from the conversation, the last of which is Catherine saying, *Cool, ok, well I'm going to go ahead and book him. Thanks for the input.* Scrolling up, I can see that they've decided as a group on the third photographer—the one I was going to vote for, too. *Sorry, was in a meeting,* I text them. *Photog looks good.* But now, of course, I look like the dummy who walks in late and starts laughing just because everyone else is.

Ten minutes later, Catherine send a quick update: *Booked! And I was thinking we could coordinate our outfits for the photoshoot?*

Mom immediately hearts the text.

LATER IN THE WEEK, a group of us are sitting in the

break room eating lunch when Luke's rugby match comes up. Apparently, the recreational team he plays on has a match this Saturday—and apparently, as his girlfriend, it's expected that I'm going.

"You *have* to go cheer him on, Emma," insists Cara, who works in Customer Support, as she dips a spoon into her yogurt.

"She really doesn't need to," says Luke.

Cara ignores him. She raises her eyebrows at me. "Trust me. Go. If you skip it, he's just going to use it against you later. He's going to be all, '*You never came to my rugby matches!*' and crap like that."

To be frank, rugby doesn't interest me. And Luke knows it, just as I know that he isn't interested in listening to me talk about Dance Den. Spending my Saturday afternoon at a rugby match—let alone cheering on a fake boyfriend—is pretty much at the bottom of my priority list. I guess I can just *say* that I'm going, though. It can be like one of our fake dates. Luke can give me the highlights afterward. It's not like I'll need to know the play-by-play.

"Sure, I'll come," I say.

"You don't have to," Luke repeats.

"No, I want to," I insist. "It'll be fun."

Luke gives me a strange look that I can't figure out the meaning of. But after lunch, after the group has broken apart, he pulls me aside and explains himself.

"You're going to have to actually come to the match, you know," he says, quietly enough that only I can hear.

"Oh I am, am I?" I say.

"Alex is on the team, too, smartypants," says Luke. "So unless you're going to bribe him or something, you can't just lie about going."

The smirk drops off my face. "He is? Since when?"

"Since last year. I talked him into joining."

Seriously? This whole time, I could have been going to their matches and had a legitimate reason for staring at Alex? I'm suddenly super annoyed with myself for not being more interested in rugby. And annoyed at Luke for never mentioning it until now.

"Well," I say, shrugging, playing it cool. "I guess I'm just going to have to actually show up. I mean, it's fine. I can watch *one* game of rugby. How long does it usually last? An hour or something?"

"How generous of you," says Luke. "And it's ninety minutes."

I SHOW up right before the match starts on Saturday. There's a small crowd already there. And as I move through the crowd, trying to find a good spot to watch from, I see a familiar face among the rest.

Alex is on the sidelines. In his street clothes, for some reason. Seeing him standing there makes my heart beat a little faster. I take a breath and sidle up beside him.

"Hey," I say, in a voice that's obviously trying to sound casual.

Alex glances at me for about a millisecond. "Oh, hey. What's up?"

"Not much," I say. "Just here to...cheer Luke on, you know." I take a second to scan the players out on the field and pick him out among them. Then I look over at Alex again. "Why aren't you out on the field?"

Alex sighs. "I screwed up my ankle yesterday. Decided to sit out today."

"Oh. That sucks. I'm sorry." Inside, though, selfishly, I'm thrilled about this turn of events. Who cares about *watching* Alex when I can *hang out* with him?

The referee blows his whistle out on the field and the game begins. I watch for a few minutes, completely at a loss.

"So, not to be annoying," I say, leaning toward Alex, "but...how does this work, exactly?"

"It's kind of like football," says Alex, keeping his eyes on the field. "You can carry, pass, or kick the ball. You can't pass it forward, though. Only backward."

"Gotcha," I say.

I return my attention to the game and continue to watch for another few minutes. But even with Alex's explanation, I can't get into it. Especially not with my crush standing right there. I just wish I could actually flirt with him—I have to keep reminding myself that I can't. Each time a flirtatious inclination strikes me, this other little stupid voice says, *You have a fake boyfriend, remember?*

"Luke said you joined the team this year?" I ask.

"Uh...yep," says Alex distractedly.

"Did you ever play as a kid?"

"No," says Alex, his eyes following the ball. "Just other sports."

"Cool, cool," I say, sounding totally uncool.

As the game continues, it doesn't become any clearer to me. So I just follow along with whatever Alex does. If he cheers, I cheer too. If he yells something out at the referee, I...well, I don't yell at the referee. But I shake my head strongly in disapproval. And then I sigh, and turn to Alex, and say something like, "What is that ref's *deal*?"

"I know," grunts Alex.

God, he's even cuter when he's mad.

I know it's wrong. I know I shouldn't. But I can't pass up such a good opportunity to try to make a connection with Alex. I mean, when am I going to have a chance like this again? Even if I come to another one of their games, his ankle will probably be fine by then. I'll be standing alone on the sidelines, watching him with faraway longing, kicking myself for not taking advantage when I could.

And so, the next time Alex says something even *remotely* funny, I laugh and gently touch his arm. It's the briefest of gestures. A quick touch. A graze, practically.

But it's enough to make him finally look over at me.

As my eyes and Alex's meet, I wait for the magical

moment to happen. I wait for him to finally realize that I've had a thing for him this whole time. But when our eyes do meet, there's nothing. Just a half-second of dull eye contact.

There is not, to my great disappointment, a single spark.

And then both of our attentions are pulled away by a succession of shrill, forceful blows of the referee's whistle. It's different than the chirps that have accompanied the game so far.

This time, it's a sound of distress.

I pivot my attention from Alex to the field. Everyone has crowded around two players who are both lying flat on the grass. Slowly, one of them gets up on his own, and nods as others presumably ask him if he's okay. The second player, though, is still down.

It takes me a second, between my slightly dazed state and the other players obscuring him, but then I realize that Luke is the second player—the one who looks like he really got knocked out. My hands rise to my mouth.

"Oh my God. Is he okay?" I ask though the screen of my fingers, not taking my eyes from Luke.

"Stay here," Alex says, and starts jogging across the field.

I want to go, too. But I know I won't be of any help. I'll just get in the way. And so, helplessly, from the sidelines, I stand and watch, feeling a terrible sourness rise in my throat. I glance around, desperately searching the faces of other people, trying to gauge how serious this is. But the worry I see in other faces only makes me freak out more.

"Did you see what happened?" I choke out to a stranger a few feet away from me. I've managed to lower my hands from my mouth, but now I can't get them to stop shaking.

"They ran headfirst into each other," he says, shaking his head. "Looked like a pretty bad hit. Oh. There he goes. He's up."

I turn just in time to see Luke stand up. I watch as the other players around him give him some breathing room. My chest half-relaxes as he takes a few steps.

He seems okay. A little wobbly. But it seems like he's doing okay.

Then he takes a few more steps, slows to a stop, bends over, and vomits onto the grass.

6

ALEX DRIVES Luke to the hospital. I follow behind in my car, my hands refusing to stop shaking as they grip the steering wheel. Logically, I know that I had nothing to do with Luke's injury, but the illogical part of me has me filled with guilt for trying to flirt with Alex. The illogical part of me has me convinced that if I hadn't been doing that, somehow Luke would still be out there on the field right now, unscathed.

Between traffic and my semi-panicked driving, I manage to lose Alex and Luke along the way. And then of course I take a wrong turn, and drive for blocks in the wrong direction before realizing my mistake. By the time I get to the hospital, I'm nearly in tears. I'm already convinced that Luke is dead—and that it's all my fault.

I find Alex in the emergency room waiting area. He tells me that Luke has been admitted.

Still shaking, I take a seat beside Alex. "How was he in the car?"

"Confused," says Alex. "I'm pretty sure he has a concussion. And his forehead was bleeding. But I don't think it was that bad."

I nod. A concussion. Of course. I don't know why I hadn't thought of that. I was in too much of a state, I guess.

"The doctor said they'd run some tests and then give us an update." Alex glances at me. "You okay?"

"Yeah, I think so," I say. I avoid his eyes and instead look around, taking in the bright white of the waiting room, the tired and worried looking people waiting to be admitted, the big red signs that read EMERGENCY. "I just don't like hospitals."

"Not many people do," Alex says.

"Doctors do," I say.

I'm not even trying to be funny. It just comes out of my mouth. But Alex laughs.

"True," he says.

Part of me wants to keep talking to Alex. Part of me wants to make him laugh again. But the other part of me is screaming in my head, *What kind of idiot are you? Did you already forget what happened the last time you tried to flirt with him?*

Reluctantly, I give into the illogical screaming voice. I lean back in the uncomfortable waiting area chair and think of Luke. I've never been a big believer of magical thinking, but right now, it feels like the only thing I can do.

Do not flirt with Alex. Do not even think about flirting with Alex. Focus on sending healing thoughts to Luke.

I'm in the middle of sending approximately my hundred-and-twentieth healing thought to Luke when a nurse comes into the waiting area and calls out Alex's name. We both quickly stand and go over to her.

"You can see your friend now," she says. "Follow me, please."

She leads us into the treatment area, which makes my heart race as soon as we enter it. We're suddenly surrounded by the insistent clicks and beeps of machines, the moaning of patients in distress, the low murmuring between doctors and nurses. When we finally reach Luke's bed, I'm beyond relieved to see him sitting upright. He doesn't look as bad as I was anticipating. He *does* have a small bandage on the side of his forehead. But besides that, he looks okay.

"Hey you," I say, sidling up next to the bed. I feel the urge to hug him, but I'm also too self-conscious to. So instead, I just awkwardly touch his arm. In response, Luke looks up at me and smiles. But it's a different kind of smile than he normally gives me. It's spacey.

That said, I'm still a little spacey, too. I'm just now realizing that there's a doctor standing on the other side of Luke's bed.

"I'm Dr. Metcalf," he says, extending a hand toward me.

"Emma," I say, shaking it. "I'm...um, Luke's girlfriend."

"Girlfriend," repeats Luke, and smiles again at me. Oh, God. Don't blow our cover, Luke.

"I'm Alex," says Alex, shaking the doctor's hand.

The doctor nods. "Right. Well, Luke has a concussion, all right. But the good news is that when we did the scan, we didn't see any internal bleeding or swelling of the brain. To recuperate, he's simply going to need lots of rest. We do recommend, however, that there's someone around to monitor him for the next forty-eight hours. Is one of you able to do that? Or another friend or family member?"

The question hangs in the air unanswered. It finally occurs to me that both the doctor and Alex are waiting for me to reply. I *am* the girlfriend, after all.

"I, um..." I glance at Alex, then back at the doctor. "We'll figure something out."

"Good. We'll be discharging him shortly, then."

The doctor quickly goes over what we need to know about post-concussion care, asks if we have any questions, and then leaves. After he goes, Luke scratches his forehead—the non-injured side—and says, "Hey, did we win?"

"The match?" says Alex. "We left early, dude."

"We left early?" asks Luke, frowning.

"You got hurt."

"Oh," says Luke. For whatever reason, he turns to look at me. "What happened?"

I feel guilty all over again that I can't describe to him exactly what happened—that I was busy trying to flirt with Alex instead of paying attention to the game.

"You collided with another player," I say. "From the other team."

"Huh," says Luke. Thankfully, he seems satisfied enough with that.

I look over at Alex. "So, uh—the next forty-eight hours, huh?"

"About that," says Alex. "I would totally do it, but I actually have a bunch of family stuff going on later today. Are you cool with staying with him?"

"Oh," I say. "Uh…"

"I'll give you my number. If it's too much to handle, you can give me a call."

I find myself nodding. I find myself saying *okay*. And the next thing I know, Luke is being discharged from the hospital, and the three of us are walking out of the building. Outside, in the parking lot, Luke squints at the sunlight. He staggers a little as Alex and I lead him to my car.

After we get him into the passenger seat, Alex pats the top of my car and says, "All good?"

"I think so," I say. I think about Alex's number, which is now in my phone. The part of me that can't help it wonders whether I'll get to use it someday for non-Luke purposes. Then my attention snaps back to the task at hand.

I ask Luke what his address is, then type it into my phone. As we drive away, I glance in the rearview mirror to see if Alex is still standing there. But he's already gone.

7

"SO THIS IS YOUR PLACE, HUH?" I say. We've just gotten to Luke's apartment. It's a pretty typical looking bachelor pad for a thirty-year-old. Everything's either gray or dark wood. He doesn't own a single plant. There's two framed pieces of art on his wall, and they're both old sports posters.

"You don't seem to approve," he says, smiling tiredly.

I shrug. "No. It's not that. It's just so...bachelor-y."

"How so?"

"I mean...the furniture? The color scheme? The fact that your windows don't have curtains?"

"Well, if I ever want to de-bachelorize the place," Luke says, "I'll know who to call."

I snort. "Yeah. I guess." If this apartment is ever going to be de-bachelorized, though, I'm sure it's going to be done by one of Luke's future girlfriends, not me.

Luke walks over to his gray couch and sinks down into it with a soft groan. Right. I'm here to be a good friend, not poke fun at his decor.

"How are you feeling?" I ask.

"Headachy. Can you get me some aspirin? It's in the bathroom."

I mentally rewind to the instructions the doctor rattled off. "Actually, the doctor said no aspirin. Something about a higher risk of bleeding, I think. I could get you something to drink, though. Do you have tea?"

"Never mind. I'll just take a nap."

"You sure?"

Luke nods and then lets his head fall back against the couch.

"Just pretend I'm not here," I say.

"Will do."

While Luke naps, I sit down in the armchair across from him and stare at my phone for a while. Eventually, though, the combination of the quiet room and the sunlight streaming in through his living room windows lulls me into a sleepy state, too. I put my phone down and lean my head back. I let my eyes close. The deliciousness of a mid-afternoon nap is too tempting to resist. Anyway, what else have I got to do?

Later, when I wake, the first thing I feel is drool at the corner of my mouth. I quickly wipe it away. I look over at Luke and blink a few times. Luckily, he's not awake yet. But as soon as I stir, he begins to wake up, too. He yawns, rubs his eyes, then opens them and meets my gaze.

"Hey," I say. "How are you feeling now?"

"Better," he says.

"Good."

He starts to get up, but I beat him to it.

"What do you need?" I ask. "I'll get it for you."

"Water would be great. Thanks."

"Sure thing."

I go into his kitchen, find his drinking glasses in the third cabinet I check, and bring him back a full glass. He drinks half of it in one go, then sets it on a side table.

"So," says Luke, shifting on the couch, "did you like watching the match?"

I sit back down in the armchair. "Yeah. It was fun. Up until the point when you got hurt, of course."

"I promise that's not how it usually goes."

"God. I hope not."

Luke smiles. "Concussion aside, at least I finally got you to come to a match. Kinda wish it didn't take a fake relationship to make it happen, but whatever."

"I would have come to one before if you'd asked me to," I say.

"I've invited you before."

"No, you haven't."

"I'm pretty sure I have."

"Pretty sure you haven't."

"Okay," he says, rolling his eyes. "Well, if you feel

like coming to any in the future, you're now officially invited."

"Noted," I say. "Hey, you know what you *should* do, after this whole fake relationship of ours is over? Invite *Erin* to a match. And then have yourself another little concussion. She'll totally fall for you then."

Luke laughs lightly. "Yeah. Maybe."

I don't know why I just suggested what I did.

A few moments of silence pass between us.

"How long have you liked her for?" I ask.

"I dunno. A while."

"A *while*?"

"Yeah. A while."

Okay. Whatever. If he doesn't want to tell me, fine. It's not like it matters. I'm just making conversation.

"Well, you've done a good job at hiding it," I say. "I had no idea."

Luke just shrugs.

A gnawing feeling tells me that I should change the subject. But now, with Luke being so evasive, my curiosity has been piqued. "How long has it been since you've had a girlfriend? And don't say 'a while.'"

Luke's eyes travel to the ceiling, like the answer is up there. "It's been several years."

"Years? Your last ex must have messed you up bad."

"No. It wasn't like that. We split up on pretty good terms."

"Then why haven't you had a girlfriend since?"

Luke runs a hand through his hair. "It's not like I

haven't dated. I just haven't met anyone that I want to keep seeing."

"Right..."

"You can stop giving me that judgy look."

"I'm not giving you a judgy look."

"Yes, you are," Luke says. "Anyway, you're not exactly in a position to judge, are you, Armstrong? You've been single for as long as I've known you."

"Yeah, but—"

"What's up with that, huh? Do *you* have an ex who scarred you or something?"

"No."

"Okay. So what's your excuse, then?"

"I haven't met the right person, either," I say.

"No. You can't say the same thing as me. I can tell you're lying, anyway."

We have a mini stare-off. I lose.

"Fine," I say. "If you really want to know the truth, I do like someone."

"And you haven't asked him out because...?"

"I just can't."

I've thought about it plenty, though, of course. I've imagined countless scenarios where I finally walk up to Alex and admit to him that I like him. But every time I think about actually asking him out, that stupid little voice in my head pipes up. *He'll say no. Of course he'll say no. Stick with oogling—damn it, ogling—him from afar. Besides, imagine how awkward it will be at the office if you go out for a while and then break up.*

"I'm not a relationship person," I say.

"What's that mean?"

"It means what it sounds like. Relationships aren't for me."

Luke gives me a half-confused, half-frustrated look. Then, finally, he says, "Okay. We don't have to talk about it if you don't want to talk about it."

"Good," I say.

I POP out that evening to grab a few things from my apartment—like my sleeping clothes and my toothbrush—and also to pick up some groceries while I'm out. Luke is in the shower when I get back to his place; the sound of the running water blooms through the apartment. I search around his kitchen for the necessary pots and utensils and things, and then get to making dinner. I've decided to make one of my favorite comfort foods: a baked penne casserole topped with heaps of cheese.

"Smells *amazing*," says Luke, when he comes into the kitchen after his shower. "Thanks for doing all this."

"I hope you like it," I say, crouching down to peek through the oven window. The cheese has just started to brown. "A couple more minutes and it'll be done."

Since Luke doesn't have a dining table, we eat at his kitchen bar. The penne, to my delight, has turned out pretty damn good. Luke compliments me numerous times about how delicious it tastes.

"You trying to butter me up or something?" I say.

"Just telling it like it is," he says.

When we're done eating, he reaches for my empty plate and stacks it on top of his. But when he tries to start cleaning up the kitchen, I tell him to cut it out.

"You're supposed to be resting," I say. "Doctor's orders."

"I think you just like saying 'doctor's orders.'"

"Maybe. But that doesn't mean it's not true."

"Okay, okay." He finally steps away from the sink.

I rip off a length of foil from a roll I find in one of his drawers, press it over the leftovers, and find a place for them in his fridge. When I close the door, I find Luke standing there, looking at me.

"You know," he says, "I've been meaning to say, I'm sorry you got roped into doing this. I realize you probably wouldn't be here right now if not for the fake relationship thing."

I shrug. "It's not a big deal. Although, for the record, you *so* owe me one now."

"How am I doing, by the way?"

"What do you mean? Like, post-concussion-wise?"

"No, I mean, as your fake boyfriend."

"You're doing fine," I say. "These couple weeks are for *your* benefit, though, remember? You're the one with a girl to impress. I should be asking you how *I'm* doing."

"I guess that's true," says Luke.

"So? How *am* I doing?"

"I have no complaints."

"I'm acting girlfriend-y enough?"

Luke smiles and nods. "You are."

"Okay. Good."

I approach the sink, squeeze dish soap onto a sponge, and start to wash our dishes. Luke has a dishwasher, but right now, I want to have something to do with my hands. There's sort of an awkward vibe in the room, and it's being made worse by the two of us just standing there.

"You can tell me, you know," he says.

I glance over at him. I don't understand. "About...?"

"About your feelings. It's okay."

I'm still confused. Then, suddenly, our conversation from earlier comes flooding back, and I understand. Luke thinks that I like *him*. He thinks *that's* the reason for my vagueness and reluctance to talk about my crush earlier.

"Oh my God, no," I say. "That's not—Luke, I don't—" Inexplicably, I start to laugh. It's not that the situation is funny. It's as if my body doesn't know what else to do.

I try to repress the laughter. I rinse off a plate and set it in the drainboard. "I don't have feelings for you."

"You don't have to be embarrassed about it," says Luke.

"I'm not embarrassed. There's nothing to be embarrassed about." I frown at him. "Honestly. I don't like you like that."

"Okay," he says.

That sort-of-awkward vibe from before? Yeah, now it's *way* more awkward.

After a few minutes, Luke says, "I'm going to call it a night. You're okay on the couch?"

"Sure," I say. "Is it cool if I stay up a while longer, though?"

"Stay up as long as you want," he says.

"Okay. Goodnight."

"Night," he says, without looking at me, and then retreats to his bedroom.

After I finish cleaning up the kitchen, I make myself a cup of tea—black tea, since that's all that Luke has—and then go into the living room and settle into the couch. I watch television until I start to feel drowsy. Before I get too drowsy, though, I go into the bathroom to get ready for bed. I wash my face, brush my teeth. I accidentally knock a container of Luke's pomade off the counter, barely missing the toilet. Then I head back to the living room.

I don't sleep super well that night. Luke's couch might be stylish, but it doesn't exactly excel in the comfort department. I make do, though. And when I wake up in the morning, I feel refreshed enough to cook breakfast for the two of us.

Before long, Luke comes out of his bedroom. He sits down at the kitchen bar and thanks me when I set a plate of eggs and french toast in front of him.

"Looks good," he says. But there's something off in his voice.

"You sleep okay?" I ask.

"Not really," he says.

"Does your head still hurt?"

"Not anymore," he says. "It did last night, though."

"Sorry," I say.

I make a plate for myself and sit down next to him.

"You were being kind of loud out here, you know," he says.

I glance at him. "This morning?"

"And last night."

"Really? Sorry. I thought I turned the television down low enough."

Luke shrugs. He doesn't look at me. He just stares down at his plate and pokes his eggs around with his fork. And suddenly I'm so annoyed with him. Why didn't he come out and tell me last night if the television was too loud? Why does he have to pick at his breakfast? What is he, a little kid?

"I'm feeling a lot better today," says Luke. "You don't need to stay any longer."

To be honest, I don't want to stick around any longer, either. Not with his weird moodiness. It does make me a little nervous to leave him alone, though.

"I don't know, Luke. Are you sure? And what about your car? We still need to go get it from the parking lot."

"I'll ask Alex to bring me over there." He's still not looking at me. "Really. You should go."

Ten minutes later, I pack up my things. I tell him I'm going to text him throughout the day to check in on him; I make him promise that he'll get in contact with me right away if he starts feeling worse. I don't like leaving with things still weird between us, but in the moment, it doesn't feel as if there are any other options.

And so I go.

8

LUKE IS like some kind of hero when he shows up to work on Monday. If you ask me, though, everyone is way too enthralled with his stitches. When I pass by his desk on the way to the copier, there's a small crowd gathered, hearing him tell his story again.

"God, how scary, Luke," says Lucinda. "Thank goodness Emma was there to look after you."

"Do you think that cut's going to leave a scar?" Derek asks, touching his own forehead.

As for me, I don't talk to Luke very much that day. Just the bare minimum to make it seem like nothing's up with the two of us. But in truth, I'm still put off by the way he acted yesterday.

And as the week goes on, I find new things to be annoyed with him about—the way his gaze slightly lingers on Erin from Accounting, the way he talks too much in a meeting, even the way he mixes sugar into his coffee. It's like all of a sudden he's gone from being my closest friend in the office to being *that annoying office guy*.

I know it's just me still feeling irritated about last weekend.

But it gives me second thoughts about this whole thing.

IT'S LATER in the week when Catherine texts me again about Hawaii. *I was thinking it would be nice to do something extra special for Mom and Dad?*

Sure, I text back. *Any ideas?*

It's a dumb question. Of course Catherine has ideas. That's like asking a millipede if it has legs. And, indeed, about a thousand options come pouring in once I ask, each one with a corresponding link. Parasailing, private chefs...the links go on and on. I mean, really. Does Catherine not realize that I'm at work? Is *she* not at work?

Actually, knowing her, she's probably just honed the ability to simultaneously text with one hand and do all her stupid lawyer things with the other.

I wait fifteen minutes, during which I get some actual work done, then pick my phone up again and pick out a link at random.

The luau sounds nice, I text Catherine.

Already reserved spots, Catherine replies. *For all of us.*

Okay, so then why did she send the link to me? Is she trying to emphasize how much work she's already put into the trip?

Cool, I text back.

Catherine doesn't type anything in response, but I can feel her waiting. It's like some kind of screwed-up test where there's a right answer and I have to keep guessing until I get it right.

I'm sure they'll love any of those options, I text her.

A few minutes later, Catherine replies, *K thanks.*

It seems our conversation is over, so I go back to work. I keep thinking about my parents' anniversary, though. Thirty years. It's sort of—no, it *is*—amazing how long they've been together. Thirty whole years. Thirty *real* years.

The true ridiculousness of my fake relationship hits me like a tidal wave.

At the end of the workday, I wait until the office mostly clears out, then I go over to Luke's desk.

"Hey," I say.

"Hey," he says, keeping his eyes on his monitor.

"Can I talk to you for a second?"

He quickly finishes up whatever he's in the middle of and swivels in his chair to face me. "What's up?"

I draw in a breath and let it out. "I just wanted to say, you don't have to come along on the trip if you don't want to."

Luke frowns. "What are you talking about?"

I brush a nonexistent crumb from the top of his cubicle wall. "I'm saying we can call it quits anytime. I'm giving you an out."

"I'm not looking for an out," he says.

"It's okay if you are."

"What's going on, Armstrong?"

I shrug. I consider telling him about my parents' anniversary, but for whatever reason, I don't. "Ever since last weekend, things have been…weird between us."

Luke looks away from me. "I've just been busy this week. I had a deadline move up."

Okay. I guess we're never going to talk about last weekend, then.

"I still want to go," says Luke.

"Are you sure?"

He nods. He smiles, instantly deflating the tension. "Besides, you really think I'm going to pass up a free trip to Hawaii?"

I smirk. "Right."

"Or pass up the chance to see you in a bikini?"

I know it's only a joke. But my cheeks involuntarily flush. "Very funny."

"Don't worry," says Luke. "I'll be right there next to you in my Speedo."

"All right," I say, rolling my eyes. "I'm heading out. See you tomorrow."

"Do you think I should pack my blue one or my

purple one?" he asks.

"For the love of God, neither," I say.

"Your loss," says Luke.

I look at him one last time to give him an exasperated look. But when our eyes meet, something inexplicable happens—it's like there's this little flicker between us. A flicker that runs up my body. A flicker that reminds me of that moment in the bowling alley.

"See you," I say, quickly pulling my eyes away.

"Later," says Luke.

I hurry to my desk to grab my bag. Along the way, I run into a chair and nearly fall over it.

"Watch out for those chairs," Luke calls out.

"Shut up," I call back.

But I can't help but laugh.

EVENTUALLY, of course, word gets out at the office that Luke and I are going on vacation together. And suddenly everyone is smiling at us in this super annoying, cloying way. They smile at us as if we've just announced that we're running off to get married—or, at the very least, that we're in love.

"Hawaii is so *romantic*," Lucinda says to me at lunch. "You two are going to have the best time."

"We're looking forward to it," I say.

"Beau proposed to me in Hawaii, you know. And

we hadn't been dating that long, either. Just like the two of you."

"Is that so," I say.

"Oh, Emma," says Lucinda, cartoon hearts practically floating up around her head, "wouldn't that be *amazing* if you came back engaged?"

Okay. I admit it. I feel pretty bad that we're lying to our coworkers. Yeah, it's just a dumb relationship. But still. With every additional day that passes, I feel more and more guilty about it. And I've been looking more and more forward to our post-vacation breakup, when things will go back to normal.

Well, I guess it won't be *normal* normal. Not right away. For a while, Luke and I will have to act freshly broken up—amicably broken up, but broken up nonetheless. For a while, we'll have to fake just the right amount of awkwardness around each other. After that, though, things can go back to normal. The two of us can go back to being just friends, he can go back to pursuing Erin from Accounting again, and I can go back to...well, my normal life.

Which sounds perfectly fine to me.

Later that same week, I'm in the middle of working on a report at my desk when I look up and see Paige's grinning face hovering over my cubicle wall. I flinch, caught off guard. Why does Paige have to act so weird all the time?

"Yes?" I say. "Can I help you?"

"I have something for you," she says.

Please don't let it be something edible. Please don't let it be something edible.

Thankfully, it's not. But I can't tell *what* it is. The object that Paige is holding up is no bigger than the size of her hand. It's rectangular. It's neon red. It's...

"An umbrella," Paige says. "For your trip."

"Oh," I say, taking it from her. "Um, thanks."

She *does* know that we're going to Hawaii, right?

"As you can see," continues Paige. "It's very, very compact. You'll be amazed, though, Emma, by how much it expands when you open it up. Go ahead, give it a try."

"I'll take your word for it," I say.

"No, really! Open it up. I want to make sure it's working okay. It's been a while since I've used it, and you know how umbrellas can get. I'd feel bad if I let you borrow it only for it to malfunction."

I stand up, because I can see that she's going to keep insisting if I don't, and hold the tiny umbrella up in the air. I press the button on it with my thumb. The umbrella emits a faint click and then expands to an admittedly impressive size, immediately shading the space around me.

Everyone around us turns to look. Everyone except for Paige gives me a look that says, *Um, why did you just open an umbrella indoors?*

Quickly, I close the umbrella.

"Thanks again," I tell Paige.

"No worries," she says. "Fun fact: *petrichor* means the smell of the rain."

* * *

I SPEND the week before our trip prepping for it. I write up a packing list, then a shopping list. I buy new sunscreen. I buy new lip balm with SPF. I do a practice pack, just to make sure everything fits in my luggage—including the umbrella from Paige. Three days before we leave, I call my credit card companies to let them know when and where I'll be. Afterward, I remind Luke to do the same.

"Okay, Mom," he says.

Well, fine. I won't try to be helpful, then.

The day before our trip, I take pictures of my credit cards and driver's license, just in case, and then settle into the couch and let my television drone on in the background while I give myself a pedicure. It actually turns out pretty decent, if I say so myself. I only have to redo two of my toes.

That night, when I get into bed, I feel as ready as I'm ever going to be. There is absolutely nothing left to do but sleep. But sleep, apparently, is the one thing my body refuses to do. All I can do is lay there, overwhelmed by anxiety. What the hell do I think I'm doing? This whole thing is crazy. It's never going to work. And Luke is already getting on my nerves—how am I going to fake being into him for the next week? There's no way my family's going to buy it. Not to mention that either Luke or I will probably slip up and say something that gives it all away.

You need to call this whole thing off, I tell myself. Drowsily, I reach for my phone.

But whatever I think I'm going to do, I fall asleep before I can do it.

9

LUKE IS ALREADY in the Uber when it picks me up the next morning. And by morning, I mean the cruel hour of 4 a.m. As I drag my stiff zombie body out to the car, I curse myself for booking us an early morning flight. And for living so far away from the airport. And for agreeing to share an Uber with Luke, because it means I can't nap my way through the ride.

I lower myself into the back seat and mumble good morning to Luke. He replies with a much-too-chipper good morning back at me. When I glance over, I see that he is irritatingly well-rested. Not a smidge of puffiness under his too-alert eyes.

"Did you go to bed yesterday afternoon or something?" I say, fighting off a yawn.

"Nine o'clock," he says.

"Sleeping pills?"

He laughs. "I went for a long run after dinner. That

wiped me out. It's what I always do when I have to get up extra early."

"Aren't you smart," I say dryly.

At least our driver isn't chatty. In fact, he says a grand total of six words: *good morning, what airline?*, and *safe travels*.

Five-star rating earned.

It's a quarter to five when we get to the airport, a bit after six by the time we get through security. After we put our shoes back on—Luke, of course, has worn very easy-to-slip-on shoes, while I'm wearing strappy sandals that take eons to put back on—Luke cracks his neck and says, "You hungry? Want to find some breakfast?"

"God yes," I say.

Ten minutes later, we're in the food court surveying our options. Only a few of the vendors are open yet, since it's still so early, and of those open, there's clearly one that's the most popular. Our fellow early morning travelers have formed a curving line leading up to it that has begun to encroach on a neighboring vendor's space.

"Looks like breakfast burritos," says Luke. "I'm going to get one of those. You?"

"I think I'm just going to get coffee and a muffin or something," I say, blinking blearily toward the coffee place on the other side of the food court.

Without another word, we go our separate ways. I stumble across the food court and get in line. I assume that I'll be done way faster than Luke. But of course there's some new guy working the counter who has to ask his supervisor a question every ten seconds, and then there's some problem with the register, and by the time it's my turn to order, Luke already has his breakfast burrito in hand and has picked out a table for us.

And he is...*flirting?*...with the woman sitting at the next table over? From here, it sure looks that way. He's flashing that stupid smile of his. Making her laugh. Making her tuck her hair behind her ear.

"Ma'am?" the barista says.

I snap out of it. I return my attention to the barista. "Right," I say. "An Americano, please. With an extra shot." My eyes roam over the display case. I catch a distorted reflection of myself, with my horribly messy topknot and puffy morning face. "And a blueberry muffin."

Luke is still talking to the woman when I walk up to the table a few minutes later. He doesn't even notice me approach. I clear my throat and pull out a chair, dragging the feet on the tiles.

"Hey," he says, straightening up in his chair. "Got your coffee?"

"Uh huh," I say, sitting down.

"Good. I was worried something was wrong. It was taking you a while."

I glance at the woman at the next table over, but she's pretending like she's in the middle of reading something very interesting on her phone. I lean across the table and whisper to Luke, "What do you think you're doing?"

"What do you mean?" he asks. He sinks his teeth into his burrito, clearly taking a huge bite to buy himself time.

"You were *flirting*," I whisper.

He chews and swallows. "I don't know what you're talking about."

"I know what I saw."

He stares at me for a second, then lowers his voice to a whisper, too. "This is fake, remember?"

"Fine," I say, leaning back. "Flirt away." I rip off a piece of blueberry muffin and chew it furiously. I know I'm acting childish, but I'm running on three hours of sleep.

We eat in silence for a few minutes. Then Luke says, "You've got a little—" and reaches across the table and paws at my face.

I jerk away. "What are you doing?"

"You have blueberry juice or something on your face."

I grab a napkin and swipe at my cheek. "Then just *tell* me that I do."

"Jeez. Sorry."

I sigh. I really need to calm down. "No. I'm sorry. I just don't do well on such little sleep."

"I'll say."

I kick him under the table.

"Oof," he says, fake-wincing. "What have you got

on, Armstrong? Steel-toe boots?"

"Very funny."

Luke takes another bite of his burrito, chews, swallows. He wipes his mouth off with a paper napkin and clears his throat. "By the way. Just so we're on the same page. How serious is this relationship?"

"What do you mean?"

"I mean, obviously, it's serious enough to invite me along on your family vacation. But is it...I dunno. I guess I'm asking, are we in love?"

What sort of question is that? I tear off another nub of blueberry muffin and crumbs scatter everywhere.

"You really think that's going to come up?" I ask.

"Probably not. But whether or not we are will inform how I act around you."

It isn't something I've considered before. But now that he's asked the question, I know the answer. Of course I want him to act like he's in love with me. It's one thing to show off a boyfriend to my family. It's another to show off a completely smitten one.

I shrug casually. "Okay. Sure. We are."

"Roger that," says Luke, and crams the last bites of breakfast burrito into his mouth.

THE AIRPLANE IS chock-full of couples besotted with each other. I've counted at least four pairs of newlyweds. They're easy to spot, with their newly lovestruck eyes and traces of bridal makeup still aglow on the women's cheekbones. Peppered in among the newlyweds are the older couples, the empty nesters who also somehow look freshly in love.

Ugh.

I hate them all.

Because for the first time since this whole thing started, I wish I was going to Hawaii with a real boyfriend. I wish I was actually in love. On the plus side, I've got the window seat. So I have that going for me, I guess.

Twenty minutes into our flight, after the initial thrill-and-terror of liftoff has subsided and the boredom of reaching cruising altitude has arrived, two impeccably dressed stewardesses maneuver the refreshment cart down the aisle. Luke gets coffee. I ask for a can of ginger ale. After the stewardesses move on, Luke turns to me and says, "You get motion sickness?"

"No," I say, cracking open the can. "Why?"

"You're drinking ginger ale."

"It's what I always get." I shrug. "The first time I flew, when I was five or six or something, I didn't know what I wanted to drink, so my mom got a ginger ale for me. It's been my in-flight drink of choice ever since."

"Ah," says Luke, a smile creeping across his face. "I see."

"What? What's so amusing about that?"

"Nothing."

God, is he irritating. But I don't feel like getting into a whole thing with him right now. I tear open the little packet of honey roasted nuts that the stewardess handed over with the drink. There's a whopping six nuts inside, and I try to make each one last as long as possible. But soon there's nothing but nut dust left. And then not even that, thanks to a saliva-wetted finger and my own lack of dignity.

"Want the rest of mine?" Luke asks.

For a second, I think he's making fun of me. Mocking me for practically licking the inside of the packet. But then I see that he's sincerely offering me the rest of his almonds. All three of them.

"Don't you want them?" I ask.

"Nah," he says. "I'm good."

I take them from him with a mumbled thank you. We finish our refreshments in silence. After handing our trash to the stewardess and returning our trays to their upright and locked position, Luke stands up to fish through his carry-on in the overhead compartment and pulls out two small navy blue pouches.

"Neck pillow?" he says, holding one out to me as he sits back down.

"Um...sure," I say, stunned that he has packed something like this. No, make that stunned that he has packed *two* of them. Did he buy them especially for this trip? I uncinch the pouch and pull out the deflated pillow. It's impossible to tell if it's brand new or not. What am I even looking for—another woman's stray hair? A lipstick stain?

"You have to blow into it," says Luke. He flips it

around in my hands and points to the valve. "Right there."

"I know how to do it," I say. "I'm just surprised that you brought these."

He has no response. He's now too busy emptying his lungs into his own pillow. I put my lips to the plastic valve on mine and do the same. When we're done, we don our inflated pillows and settle in for the next several hours of the flight.

I, of course, end up dozing off, despite my best efforts to stay awake. It's a surprisingly pleasant nap, thanks to the soft companionship of the pillow. It feels as if hours and hours pass by. And while asleep, I have a dream that I'm sitting on top of a huge, velvety apricot, drifting through the heavens like it's the most normal thing in the world. But just as I'm about to lean down and take a bite out of the ripe flesh of the fruit, I'm woken with a jolt—then wrenched into hyperawareness by another one.

Here's something you should know about me: every time I fly, I secretly resign myself to the belief that the plane I'm on is going to crash. Yeah, I know. Statistically, flying is safer than driving, turbulence is harmless, so on and so forth. I've heard it all. But when the bumpy ride kicks in, and the Fasten Seatbelt sign lights up with that alarming little angry chime, all my rationality is blinded by panic. Suddenly, all I can think about is how insanely high up in the air we are.

I mean, why can't airplanes fly at, like, a more reasonable height?

The cabin shudders again, and instinctively, I reach out and grab Luke's hand. I'm not even thinking about the fact that it's his hand. It's just a hand, as far as I'm concerned.

"Man, look how much the wing's bouncing," says Luke.

My eyes snap open. There is no bouncing wing. Just Luke, totally unperturbed, smiling at me with amusement.

"Damn it, Luke," I murmur. I tear my hand from his. I close my eyes and lean back into the headrest, willing it to stop moving.

"We're fine," says Luke. "Stop freaking out."

"That's not helpful."

"And what would be helpful, Armstrong?"

I breathe out. "Distraction."

"Right. Want me to read aloud to you from the in-flight magazine? Tell you a knock-knock joke? Give you math equations to work out?" Then his voice gets closer. Softer. Sultry, almost. "Or, come to think of it, you know what would be a really good distraction…"

My eyes snap open. I look over at him. He's grinning like an idiot. He's just messing with me, of course. But I have to admit it. It works. I'm no longer thinking so direly about the impending catastrophe of our plane. Now I'm thinking about how disturbing it would be to join the mile high club with Luke.

Overhead, the captain comes on the intercom and assures us that there are clear skies ahead.

"Guess we missed our chance," says Luke.

"Oh, shut up," I tell him.

"Hey, I was just doing what you asked me to."

I rub my temples. "Please just stop, Luke."

Soon, as promised, the turbulence dies down. The next hour is smooth as silk. I spend most of it looking out the window, watching the clouds suspended over the ocean, grateful to be alive.

DURING THE LAST half hour of the flight, I dig my cosmetic pouch out of my carry-on and attempt to make myself look a little more decent. I'm finishing up applying blush to my cheeks when I notice that Luke is staring at me.

"What are you doing?" he asks.

"My...makeup?" I say.

"I know," he says. "But why? You looked fine."

"Gee. Thanks. I've always wanted to look fine."

Luke sighs. "I meant that you didn't need to put on that stuff. I meant that you already looked good."

"Okay, for future reference?" I say. "It's *much* better to tell a girl she looks good versus telling her she looks fine."

"You don't normally wear this much makeup at work."

"No. But I'm not at work. I'm on vacation."

"Yeah, a beach vacation," he says. "With your family. And a fake boyfriend who you don't need to impress."

I don't need to explain myself to him. And I'm certainly not going to take beauty advice from him. I begin to carefully apply eyeshadow to my lids, picking a shimmery peach tone from the mini-palette I've brought along. It's my favorite shade, even if the shimmery-ness sometimes gets into my eyes.

"What's this for?" asks Luke, pulling out a small round container from the pouch.

"It's setting powder," I say. "Just please don't—"

But he's already unscrewed the top. As soon as he opens it up, a tiny cloud of powder puffs up. While he coughs, I snatch the container away from him and screw the lid back on.

"You should warn a guy," he says, coughing again.

I roll my eyes, finish my makeup, and check it at a few different angles in a pocket mirror. If Luke hadn't just teased me for putting makeup on, I would ask him if I look okay. But I'm sure he'll make some joke about it, and I've had about enough of him already today.

To my surprise, though, Luke nudges me and say, "Hey. You look nice."

I look at him. Is he being sarcastic?

"I mean, to be fair, I think you look good either way. But the makeup or whatever looks good, too."

"Thanks," I say. He's probably just saying it because he feels bad about what he said before. But whatever.

I'll take it. I put my things away and settle back against my seat. We've just started our descent toward the islands. I gaze out the window and take a deep breath in. It's beautiful, all that ocean down there. It really is something.

I feel a ripple of nerves, though, too, thinking about the week that lays ahead. This could be such a huge disaster. Who brings a fake boyfriend along on a vacation, anyway? It isn't something normal people do.

Luke seems to sense my uneasiness. He leans closer to me. I can feel his breath gently on my neck.

"I promise this will go okay, Emma," he says.

I really, really hope he's right.

10

HAWAII IS BEAUTIFUL. I mean, of course it is. It's freakin' Hawaii. As we disembark the plane and navigate through the open-air airport, it feels as if we've stepped straight into a postcard. The sky is impeccably blue; the flora is perfectly green. Even the air feels more pure here.

Outside the airport, Luke and I stand in line for a cab among a throng of fellow tourists. The driver who picks us up is an extremely cheerful man of undeterminable age who is wearing a taffy pink Hawaiian shirt.

"First time visiting?" he asks as he merges into traffic. His smile fills up the entire rearview mirror.

"I've been once," I say, leaning toward the front seat. "It's his first time, though." I gesture toward Luke.

The driver's grin widens. "Honeymoon?"

"No," I say. We can't possibly have that look about us, can we? "Family vacation."

"Ah," he says. "Excellent. Any children?"

Is he asking if *we* have any children? Or if there are any children in the group? I guess it's the same answer either way.

"No," I say, and yawn, a wave of tiredness catching up with me.

"I've got four myself," he says.

"Oh, wow," I say. And I finally notice the photograph taped above the glovebox: a family portrait of himself with a woman I can only assume is his wife and their four children, each head at a slightly different height but all four of their faces reproducing their father's colossal smile.

I relax against the headrest and watch the scenery pass by. Palm trees sway spiritedly in the breeze. Teenagers heft their surfboards on the side of the road. Our driver points things out as he takes us up to the north side of the island, telling us the names of places, encouraging us to repeat the beautiful words after him. The Hawaiian language turns into tongue twisters in my mouth, but Luke's actually pretty good at it.

"Impressive," I say, glancing over at him.

Luke shrugs. "What can I say? I'm a talented guy."

I snort and turn my gaze back to the window.

As we pull up to the rental house, the first thing I notice is the minivan parked out front. For a second, I wonder if I've gotten the address wrong. Then I realize that the minivan is the rental vehicle my parents have decided upon.

I guess there's a first time for everything.

Our taxi eases to a stop and our driver jovially announces the fare. I start to get out my credit card, but Luke beats me to it.

"You didn't have to do that," I tell him, as we get out of the taxi. "The deal is that you're getting an all-expenses-paid vacation out of this, remember?"

"And what happens if I break one of the rules?" he asks, stuffing his wallet back into his pocket.

It's a good question. And one I don't know the answer to.

"I don't know," I say. "Just don't."

I grab the handle of my luggage and start rolling it toward the front door. It's big, this rental house. I mean, I knew it was going to be nice—Catherine texted us the listing—but in person, it's even grander. I'm even a little embarrassed about it. I wonder if I should explain to Luke that we don't always stay in places like this—that it's different this time since it's Mom and Dad's thirtieth anniversary.

Crap. Their anniversary.

Note to self: sneak away at some point and buy a gift for them.

"Everything good?" says Luke.

"Yep," I say. I step onto the welcome mat. I know I should be raising my hand to knock on the door, but suddenly I can't.

I turned to look at Luke. He returns my gaze.

"What?" he says.

"I feel the need to apologize in advance," I say. "For my family. You know how families...are."

"It'll be fine," he says. "Trust me. Parents love me."

"Met a lot of parents, have you?" I say.

He smirks. "Are you going to knock or do you want me to?"

But before either of us can, the door opens on its own. Or, rather, Mom opens the door. She's looking as lovely as always, only she's now a tropical version of herself. She's wearing a flowy tunic and slender white pants and somehow already looks like she has a tan.

"I thought I heard someone at the door," she says.

I step in to give her a hug. She smells of the perfume she's worn for decades, a scent I have searched for in department stores and have never been able to find.

"Did you have a nice flight?" she asks.

"It was fine," I say.

She turns her attention to Luke. "And you must be Luke. It's wonderful to meet you."

"It's great to meet you too, Mrs. Armstrong." Luke extends a hand, but Mom ignores it and goes in for a hug. Over her shoulder, Luke raises his eyebrows at me and mouths, *See?*

Mom pulls out of the hug and takes another look at him. "Good lord, you're handsome. I can see why my Emma likes you."

"Mom," I say, mortified.

"Well, he is, isn't he?" she says. She looks at me as if I'm actually supposed to answer the question. I grab the handle of my luggage and pull it further into the house, which is suddenly more difficult to do because one of the wheels has gone all wonky.

"Look at this place," I say. It's even more impressive, and more embarrassing, inside than out. "Can we get a tour?"

Mom shows us into the living room, which is decorated in greens and pinks and golds and looks like something out of a catalog—there's even a bowl of fake fruit placed perfectly in the center of the coffee table. Next, she shows us the dining room, which does not contain fake fruit but does feature a painting of a slightly lazy-eyed horse standing on the beach. It's one of those bizarre paintings where the eyes follow you everywhere—but only the lazy eye, in this case.

I turn to say something to Luke about it, but when I look over at him, he's busy talking to Mom.

"A blind date?" she's saying. "How funny. I didn't know young folks did that anymore these days." Then she turns to me and says, "Luke was just telling me how you two met, honey."

"Ah," I say. Blind date? Since when did we meet on a blind date?

"I want to hear more about it later," Mom says. "But for now, let's continue on with the tour. The kitchen's through here."

We follow her into the kitchen, which is surprisingly normal. No fake objects, no creepy horse paintings. Instead, there's a large window framing the surrounding view. It's breathtaking, that view. For a moment, it erases all the anxiety I have about this trip.

Lastly, we go upstairs, where all the bedrooms are.

"Dad and I took the master," Mom says, gesturing toward the end of the hall. Then she points to the bedroom door nearest to us. "Catherine and Kenneth took this room. The other two bedrooms are identical in size, so you two can pick whichever you like and Garrett will take the other."

I step into one of the rooms to take a look and then step into the other. The only difference is that one shares a wall with the room that Catherine and her husband are in. Standing there in the adjoining room, I have a flashback of arguing with my sister through our childhood bedroom walls.

"We'll take this one," I say, walking into the room across the hall. Luke follows me into the room, quickly surveys it, and nods in approval. He does a magnificent job of ignoring the elephant in the room: the bed that we are definitely not sleeping in together. I don't know what our sleeping arrangement is going to be, but I guess we'll figure that out tonight.

"Where is everyone else, by the way?" I ask.

"They're out in the yard," says Mom. "Should we join them?"

I nod. Mom turns and starts to head back

downstairs. Luke starts to walk in that direction, too. But I grab him by the wrist.

"Blind date?" I hiss.

"Well, I couldn't exactly say we met at work," he says quietly, wrenching his arm out of my death grip.

I want to smack my own forehead. He's right. We came up with a story to tell our coworkers how we got together, but we never did concoct one to tell my family. God, this whole fake relationship thing is exhausting.

"Okay," I say. "Fine. We met on a blind date. What did we do?"

Luke blows air out between his lips. "Dinner? Italian food?"

"Okay. And who set us up? A mutual friend?"

"That's generally how blind dates work."

"Okay, wise guy. Who set us up, though?"

Luke frowns at me. "Do you even have any other friends in the office?"

I grit my teeth. "If it comes up, let's just say Lucinda. Now come on. If we stay in here any longer, people will start getting ideas."

We catch up with Mom and follow her out to the back patio, which looks over a lush, sloping yard. On one end of the patio, Catherine is reclined on a deck chair, a sunhat tilted down over her face. She doesn't look an ounce pregnant. Actually, she looks even more toned than when I last saw her. The long dress she's wearing somehow both shows off her figure and looks super comfy.

"Emma and her boyfriend are here," says Mom.

Catherine lifts the hat from her face and blinks at us. She has clearly just been napping. But, being Catherine, it's an elegant nap, from which she wakes up from gracefully.

"Hey, guys," she says, and yawns tidily. Her manicured nails glint in the sun.

Luke steps forward and introduces himself. As Catherine shakes his hand, I watch her expression change. I can practically hear her thoughts, it's so obvious what she's thinking: *This is Luke? This is the dude that Emma is dating? How did she manage to snag a guy like this?*

Catherine smiles. "Luke," she says. "It's so nice to meet you. You're sort of a miracle, did you know that?"

"How so?" asks Luke, amused.

"Well, Emma hasn't introduced a boyfriend to us since...well, I can't even remember when."

Luke laughs politely. He shoots me a look that says, *Wow, okay. Nice sister.*

I breathe in, breathe out. "Where's Dad?" I ask.

"Exploring the property with Kenneth," says Mom as she polishes her sunglasses on her blouse. I gaze out over the yard and spot the two of them examining some big-leafed tree. Kenneth and my dad are both nature buffs; they can talk about that kind of stuff for days on end. It's nice that they can bond like that. I never know what to say to Kenneth. Although I guess what I would *really* love to ask him is what made him want to marry Catherine.

"Garrett's flight lands in about an hour," says Catherine. "Once he gets here, we'll eat something light and then head out to ride the horses."

"The horses?" I say, looking over my shoulder at her. Catherine is resting her hands above her head now, to give the undersides of her arms a chance to tan, I guess.

"Yes," she says, with that slightly annoyed tone I am so used to by now. "Didn't you see the itinerary that I emailed out?"

"I must have missed it."

"I sent it out, like, three days ago. Everything that I planned for the trip is in there."

I glance over at Luke, worried that this is all too much for him. The over-the-top house, the mean sister, the mother that practically swooned when she saw him. Honestly, I won't blame him if he wants to get the hell out of here.

But he looks cool. None of it seems to bother him. Even when he catches me looking at him, he just gives me a questioning look.

A speck of something makes itself known in my eye. Ugh. It's that stupid eyeshadow. I blink furiously, willing it to go away.

"Emma," says Catherine. My vision clears just in time for me to catch the bottle of sunscreen that she chucks at me. "Put some on. You're already starting to burn."

I scoff. But she's not wrong. A glance down at my pale arms tells me as much. Still, I can't bring myself to do as she says. Besides, I brought my own sunscreen, thank you very much.

"I'm going inside to take a nap," I say, and throw the bottle back at Catherine.

11

IN THE WARM BEDROOM UPSTAIRS, I set an alarm on my phone and pass out on top of the unfamiliar sheets. When I wake, I hear the soft chatter of voices downstairs and head down to find everyone eating in the kitchen.

"I hope you're going to take time off from work when the baby comes," Mom is saying.

Catherine nods. "The firm has a really generous parental leave policy. I was joking with Kenneth that he should get a job there, too, so that we can both take advantage of it."

Garrett has arrived by then, and I hug him hello. I also greet Dad and Kenneth, who are in the middle of discussing the history of sugar production.

"Hey, peanut," says Dad. It's a nickname that kind of makes me feel like I'm twelve years old again—

especially right now, in the presence of Luke—but mostly I find it endearing.

"You guys have been introduced to Luke, right?" I ask.

"We have," says Dad. He smiles. "Nice guy."

I am, of course, thrilled to get Dad's approval. Even if it's all a sham. I guess I hadn't realized it, but I'd been nervous about Luke fitting in with my family. As it turns out, though, Luke is a natural fit. Glancing over at him now, seeing him talking to Mom, he truly looks at ease.

I only get to enjoy the feeling of tranquility for a few seconds, though. Sure enough, it's quickly broken by Catherine.

"Okay, everyone," she says, raising her voice to get our attention. "We've got some horses to ride! Let's all meet out front in five."

One minivan ride later, the seven of us are filing out of the vehicle and stepping foot onto Royal Falls Ranch. It's ridiculously beautiful here. There's endless lush green terrain and views for days. Even Anthony, the tour guide assigned to us, is stunningly handsome. I feel my cheeks go warm when he shakes my hand.

Anthony tells us a little about the history of the ranch, then gives us a rundown of what to do and what not to do while we're on the tour. The laundry list of *don'ts*—for instance, don't squeeze the horse too forcefully with your legs, don't hold the reins too tight, don't slouch, don't forget to breathe—is mildly alarming.

"Everyone good?" Anthony asks, scanning the group. His eyes eventually land on me. He smiles. "Uh oh. You look concerned."

"Me? Oh. No. I'm good." I feel my cheeks heat up again. Damn it. Stop it, cheeks.

Anthony's gaze lingers on me for a half-second longer, then he asks us all to follow him into the stable to pick out our horses. I'm glad for the change of subject, but I also have no idea which one to pick. They're all intimidating, as far as I'm concerned. I swear, one horse even gives me the stink eye. *Don't even*, that horse seems to be warning me. *Pick me and I'll fling you off.*

I glance around. Everyone else has settled on a horse. They've practically already bonded with their selections.

"Need help?" Anthony asks.

I startle. I didn't notice him approach. "Uh, yeah, actually. Can you help me pick one?"

"Of course," he says. He looks me over—a look that makes me blush again—then nods. "I've got the perfect one."

The horse he shows me to is one that I must have missed. It's a slightly smaller one, a pretty thing with a speckled white and brown coat.

"This is Butterbean," says Anthony. "She'll take good care of you."

"Thank you so much," I say, reflexively playing with my hair.

Anthony helps everyone mount their chosen horse —Catherine, of course, looks like some kind of goddess up on hers—and then gets on his own and leads the way toward the trail. Our horses all seem to know to follow him, but still, it's a little scary straddling something that could break into a full-on gallop in the opposite direction if it wanted to.

As we start down the trail, Luke sidles up beside me on his horse. "Hey, maybe wipe the drool off your chin?"

"Excuse me?" I say.

"The tour guide. It's obvious you have the hots for him."

"I don't know what you're talking about," I say. I carefully squeeze my legs around Butterbean's sides, urging her to pick up the pace and carry me away from Luke's accusations, but Butterbean ignores my prompting.

"Well, at least be more subtle about it, huh?" Luke says. "You were the one who established the no-flirting rule, remember?"

"Whatever," I say, looking away.

Butterbean lurches forward, jerking me with her.

"*Butterbean*," I say sternly.

In response, she snorts and shakes out her mane.

I can't deny that the hour-long ride that follows is beautiful—we go up and down the ranch's hills, and through little shady groves, and continually get glimpses of the mountains and the ocean. After a while, though, my butt cheeks start to hurt, and my bladder starts to throb. Butterbean, too, is starting to get grumpy. Every time we have to scale another hill, I swear I hear her grumble.

Everyone else still seems to be having a fabulous time, though. Especially Luke. It's kind of infuriating how easy it is for him to impress my parents. But I tell myself that it's because he's a stranger, not their daughter. I also remind myself that he's faking having his life together.

As hesitant as Luke was when I'd first brought up wanting him to lie to my family about being an entrepreneur, he sure doesn't seem to have any qualms about it now. From the back of the pack, I overhear snippets of him telling them about the startup that he's recently launched. Apparently, he's developed some kind of marketing software, and it's going even better than he expected. Luke is talking about it so convincingly that, for a second, I even believe him myself.

On our way back, I finally get Butterbean to get her butt in gear and I catch up with Luke.

"Having fun?" I ask.

"Actually, yeah. I like your family."

"You do remember that you're here for *my* benefit, right? Not yours?"

He gives me a funny smile. "Uh, yeah?"

"So then stop—" I sigh. What am I supposed to say?

Stop being so charismatic? Stop doing such a good job at what I asked him to do?

"Hey, Armstrong? *Relax*. Enjoy yourself."

"Don't tell me to enjoy myself," I grumble. "I *am* enjoying myself."

AFTER LEAVING THE RANCH, we pile back into the minivan and head to some restaurant that Catherine says is one of the best on the island, according to her "research," which I'm sure was just reading reviews on the internet. She's right, though, of course. The food is amazing. We order, among other things, the shrimp dumplings, the blistered shishito peppers, the seared ahi tuna, the yucca fries, the guava chicken; it's all perfect cooked, perfectly plated.

I unabashedly stuff my face.

Later, back at the rental, we collectively decide to call it a night. As Luke and I return to our shared bedroom, I try to ignore the awkward feeling that follows us in.

I glance at the bed, then at Luke.

"We are not sleeping together in that thing," I say.

"Fine by me," he says.

"We can trade nights sleeping on the floor."

"That's what I was going to suggest, too," he says. "I'll take it tonight."

I grab my pajamas and toothbrush and step out of the room to use the bathroom down the hall. When I come back, Luke has changed into a white undershirt and pajama bottoms. Red pajama bottoms with reindeer on them.

"You do know it's not Christmas, right?" I say.

"I thought I grabbed a different pair," he says. "Anyway, will you stop checking me out? *Jeez.*"

I know he's just deflecting my teasing, but my face warms.

"Bathroom's all yours," I say.

While Luke is brushing his teeth, I toss one of the pillows and the top blanket from the bed onto the floor for him. Then I get into bed and try to get comfortable. By the time he comes back into the bedroom, I've found a good spot.

"You're not one of those weirdos who needs a completely dark room to sleep, are you?" he asks.

"I'm not a vampire, no," I say.

"Good," he says.

I listen as he settles down onto the floor, trying to get comfy with the blanket and pillow. I do feel a little bad. There's plenty of room in the bed. But...no. It would be too weird.

Anyway, I'm a tosser and turner when I sleep. And I'm not about to put myself at risk of tossing and turning onto Luke.

"Good night," Luke says from the floor.

"Good night," I say. I shut my eyes and pretend like he's not there.

Thankfully, it's easy to do.

12

THE FIRST THING I hear when I wake up the next morning is the sound of a dying animal. Groggily, I roll to the edge of the mattress and peer over it to find the source of the sound. Luke is sitting hunched over on the floor, rubbing his shoulder, grimacing the worst grimace I have ever seen.

"Hey," I say. "You okay?"

It's a stupid question. Of course he's not okay. I try again. "The floor messed up your back, didn't it?" Not that that's much better. Now I'm just stating the obvious.

"I'll be fine," he groans.

Taking the stairs slowly, Luke and I head down to join everyone. Mom and Catherine are finishing up making breakfast. Golden brown bacon is heaped on a plate and fluffy scrambled eggs practically hover over another. A third plate is covered with flawlessly uniform sliced fruit. The rich smell of coffee swirls around us the moment we step into the room.

"Sleep well?" Catherine asks, looking us over.

"Fine," I say. Luke nods in agreement, although I can see that grimace hiding beneath his smile. We definitely need to figure out a different sleeping arrangement for the rest of the trip.

"I hope you're hungry," says Catherine. She pops a blueberry into her mouth. "God, is this baby making me crave fruit. It's funny, though, I can't handle artificially sweet stuff now. Makes me nauseous even thinking about it."

Of *course* pregnancy would make Catherine crave healthy food.

Five minutes later, we're all seated around the table eating. I'm shoving a forkful of eggs into my mouth when Catherine brings up the nice, long hike that she has planned for us all. My eyes dart over to Luke. There's no way he's going to be able to hike with his back screwed up. And while I know I could tell everyone about Luke's problem and they would understand, I don't want to embarrass him. And I definitely, *definitely* don't want anyone thinking it was a sex injury.

I quickly swallow and clear my throat. "Actually," I say, "Luke and I were thinking about doing a couple's massage today." It's the first and only thing that comes to mind, but I have to say, it's not the worst fib I've ever come up with. Out of the corner of my eye, I see Luke give me a grateful look.

"Oh," says Catherine, faking coolness through her obvious annoyance. "Well, you two have fun."

"Be sure to take lots of pictures on the hike," I tell her.

"We will," she says, practically through clenched teeth.

WHILE LUKE and I take a cab into town, I search on my phone for places that offer couple's massages. Not that I particularly want to do a couple's massage with Luke, but I figure it's easier to just go along with it. I'm already lying enough to my family. Besides, what am I going to do, sit around while Luke's getting a massage?

"Thanks for doing this," says Luke. He sucks in a sharp breath as the cab drives over a pothole.

"No problem," I say. "I can tell your back is really bothering you."

"It's my treat, though. The massages, I mean."

"No. It's mine. It's my fault for making you sleep on the floor."

"You didn't make me do anything," says Luke. He nods his chin toward my phone. "Any luck?"

"I'm still looking," I say. "I'm sure I'll find something."

Unfortunately for me, though, it seems like everything is booked. Each phone call I make is met with the same answer: *Sorry, miss, but we don't have any availability this afternoon. Is there another day that would work for you?*

By the fifth phone call, we've reached town. The driver asks where we want to be dropped off.

"Here's fine," I say, at the same time that Luke says, "Keep driving around."

"Which is it?" the driver asks.

"Here's fine," I repeat. Why should we pay more to be driven around the block? But as soon as the cab pulls over and I watch Luke hobble out onto the sidewalk, I feel terrible all over again. I just hope there's a spa somewhere close by.

"Sorry, Luke," I murmur, and drop my eyes to my phone again, redoing the search now that we're actually in town. Damn it. There's nothing around here—well, nothing except for a spa in a five-star hotel.

"Find anything yet?" Luke asks. He rubs his neck. "God, I think that cab ride made it even worse."

"Uh, hold on," I say. I zoom out on the map. The next nearest day spa is more than ten blocks away. Oh, forget it. When else am I ever going to get a massage like this? I pull up the fancy hotel's website and call their spa's phone number. A honey-voiced woman answers after one ring.

"Hi," I say. "I know this is extremely last minute, but I was wondering if you had any availability for a couple's massage? Like, um...available now?"

"Let me check on that for you," the honey voice

says. She daintily clicks a few keys on her keyboard. "Miss? Good news. We do have something available. Would you like me to go ahead and book you for the ninety-minute couple's massage?"

"Great," I say, relieved. "Yes. Thank you." I'm too afraid to ask how much it's going to cost me, though. I hang up and muster up the cheerfulness to tell Luke the good news.

Two blocks later, we step into the fancy hotel, which is not kidding around with its fanciness. Everything about it is so...shiny. And serious. And heavy-looking. I keep expecting someone to come up to us and tell us there's been some mistake, that we clearly aren't cut out to be here. But the woman at the reception desk doesn't blink twice when I ask her where the spa is. She simply whips out a map of the property and traces a line with her perfectly manicured finger from where we currently are to where we're trying to go.

Despite her directions, we make a wrong turn—or, rather, I make a wrong turn and half-blind-with-pain-Luke follows me—but eventually we make it to the spa, where the honey-voiced woman from the phone call greets us and gives us robes and points us back to the changing rooms.

"See you in a bit, I guess," I say to Luke.

"Yep," says Luke, before hobbling away.

The women's changing room is a fog of eucalyptus-scented steam and nudity. I waste no time getting out of my clothes and into the unbelievably soft robe. I then maneuver my way past more naked women and exit the changing room to the waiting room, where Luke is relaxing in a chair as he flips through a magazine.

"You're looking better already," I say, taking a seat next to him.

"I think they're pumping something into the air here."

I laugh. "Well, whatever it is, it's working." I nod at the magazine in his hands. "You gonna subscribe?"

"Oh, definitely," he says. He angles the page toward me and taps a photo of a woman in a contortion-esque yoga post. "I'll give you a hundred bucks if you can do that."

"Two hundred."

"A hundred and fifty." He sizes me up. "Wait. You're probably really flexible, aren't you? You go to that dance thing all the time."

That dance thing. It amuses me that he doesn't remember what Dance Den is called, not to mention that he seems to think it's more disciplined than it actually is. Dance Den has made me exactly zero percent more flexible compared to when I started.

A woman comes into the waiting room and calls our names. As she leads us down the hall, she makes small talk, asking how long we're in Hawaii for, how long we've been together. When I tell her we've only been together for a few weeks, she says, "Oh, how sweet!" in a tone that she probably uses regardless of whether the answer is a day or fifty years. Then she opens a door that leads out to a wooden structure that opens onto a tropical landscape. It's a gorgeous setup.

Gorgeous and expensive-looking.

The masseuse tells us to make ourselves comfortable on the massage tables and says she'll be back in a few minutes. As soon as she leaves, I make a speedy transition between getting out of my robe and tucking myself beneath the sheets on the massage table. Which is followed by several awkward minutes of silence where both Luke and I are lying naked on our respective tables, both staring down through our headrests at the ground.

"It's nice here," I say, my smushed cheeks distorting the words.

"It is," he responds from his table.

Finally, the masseuse returns, bringing with her a second masseuse, their four shoes clapping quietly on the floor as they approach our tables. My masseuse lightly places her fingertips on my shoulders and says, "Are we ready to get started?"

With still-smushed cheeks, I say, "Uh huh."

It's been forever since I've gotten a massage, and I've forgotten how nice it is. Within seconds, I'm transported into the heavenly state that is getting your body wrung out by expert hands. The masseuse works her way from my neck to my toes and back again, ever so politely folding back the sheets and then recovering them as she does so.

When she's done with my back, she asks me to flip over, and I raise my face out of the hole and turn. As I do, I catch a glimpse of Luke also flipping over on his massage table. Only his lower half is covered by the sheets, and I see, for the first time, Luke's shirtless upper body. He's more built than I expect. I mean, it's not like I thought he was *flabby* under those slim-flit shirts he wears. But I didn't expect such a...well, a toned upper body.

Not that it matters. I couldn't care less how often Luke works out.

I settle onto my back and close my eyes and pull my attention back to the massage. I do not think about Luke's bare chest again. Not once.

When our massages are over, and we've changed back into our street clothes, we meet up back at the spa's front desk. Luke is walking upright now, without a trace of a pain on his face. As for me, I feel like a whole new, relaxed, glowy person.

"How were your massages?" the honey-voiced woman asks.

"Wonderful," I say. Even my *lips* feel new.

"Yeah, it was great," says Luke, and starts to pull out his wallet. I tell him to stop, that I'll get this, that I'm happy to take care of it. I pull out my credit card and slide it across the counter.

"Your total today is five hundred," says the honey-voiced woman. "Would you like to add a tip?"

Five hundred dollars? Is she serious? I don't—I can't even—

"We'll actually be splitting the cost," says Luke, placing his credit card firmly on the counter. "And the tip can go on my card. Let's say forty."

"Thank you, sir," says the woman.

Outside of the hotel, in the bright sunlight, I stammer out an apology. "God, Luke. I'm sorry. I didn't realize it would be *that* expensive. I wasn't expecting it to be cheap, but five hundred dollars..."

"Well, technically, it was only two-fifty each, before the tip. Practically a steal, huh?"

I blow air out between my lips.

"Come on, cheer up," says Luke. "It's not that big of a deal. Want to grab a bite to eat?"

I check my phone. There are no messages from Catherine, so it seems safe to assume that they're still on the hike.

"Sure," I say.

"Any cravings?"

"Uh...something cheap? We could grab some canned Spam or something."

I'm joking, but I'm also not.

Luke cranes his neck to look down the street. "Looks like there are a bunch of restaurants over there. Come on. Let's go see what looks good. It'll be my treat."

"Luke, you really don't have to—"

"*Stop*, Armstrong. I'm treating you to lunch, and that's final."

The way he says it makes it clear that there's nothing I can do to convince him otherwise. And so I give in. We head down the block and decide to get a table at one of the restaurants that has patio seating and happy-looking diners. Along with our food, we each order one of the big blue cocktails that everyone's drinking, which ends up tasting like happiness in a glass. By the end of our lunch, I'm even feeling glad to be here with Luke.

13

WE'VE BARELY BEEN BACK at the house for two minutes when Catherine pulls me aside and says we need to talk.

"What's *wrong* with you?" she says in a loud whisper. "Why'd you have to go get a couple's massage?"

I shrug. "What's the big deal?"

"I'm gifting a surprise couple's massage to Mom and Dad."

"Um, okay?" I say. "So?"

"So, it doesn't make it as special if you and your boyfriend decide to go out and get one on a whim. It makes it seem like their surprise is an afterthought."

"Catherine, come on. I didn't know. Besides, you're overthinking—"

"You *would have* known if you'd read the itinerary that I emailed out."

I roll my eyes. How can I not?

"Oh, forget it. You're impossible," she says, and storms out.

Catherine and I avoid each other for the rest of the day. With the house the size it is, it's easy enough to do. The rest of the day passes by at a leisurely pace: we all hang out in the yard, we drink beers, we crack open a coconut that falls from one of the palm trees. Luke and Garrett have a long conversation about sports that I listen to briefly before tuning out. Dad asks me about work, and I shrug and say that it's pretty much the same as always, then ask how things are going with the restaurant. We eat dinner outside that night, a meal of fish tacos and more beers.

Later that evening, returning to our bedroom, Luke and I look at each other and then at the floor.

"I'm not going to make you sleep on the floor," Luke says. "You can take the bed again."

"Are you out of your mind?" I say. "Do you not remember how screwed up your back was today?"

"Well, what do you propose, then? Should I go sleep in the minivan?"

For a second—a split second—I consider saying yes.

Instead, I say, "We can share the bed. Just...stay on your side, and I'll stay on mine."

"Okay," says Luke. "That works."

And so I get into one side of the bed, and he gets into the other. I'm so close to the edge of the mattress that if I roll in my sleep, I'll fall off. But the mere thought of moving any closer to Luke makes my stomach twist, so I stay on the edge, say a quick silent prayer that I will stay absolutely still during the night, and shut my eyes.

I'M TOTALLY disoriented when I wake up the next morning. I'm not even aware that I'm in Hawaii. All I'm aware of is the fact that I'm in a bed, and that my leg is touching someone else's.

It's been a long, *long* time since I've woken up next to anyone in bed. And in my disorientated state, all I can think about is how nice it is to have a little physical contact. You miss it, you know? So I lay there like that for several minutes, enjoying the skin-on-skin sensation, until it finally occurs to me who's leg is touching mine.

I jerk my leg away and jolt up in bed. Thankfully, beside me, Luke is still sound asleep. As quietly but as quickly as I can, I get out of bed, grab some fresh clothes from my suitcase, and leave the bedroom to go take a shower.

When I get back to the bedroom, Luke is awake, still in bed but scrolling through his phone. He sets it down for a minute and yawns and says, "God, that was so much better than sleeping on the floor."

I make a sound in my throat and busy myself with stuffing yesterday's clothes in the plastic bag that I brought for dirty clothes.

"You sleep okay?" he asks.

"Yep," I say. I grab my phone. "I'm going downstairs."

Luke yawns. "All right," he says. "See you down there."

There's no smorgasbord of breakfast waiting today, just cereal and milk and fruit. While we eat, Catherine presents several options for activities that day. We take a vote and settle on the beach. It's not until the vote is over that it occurs to me that going to the beach means seeing Luke's half-naked body again—a thought that once I have, I inexplicably can't get out of my head.

LUCKILY, though, when we *do* get to the beach, I manage to avoid looking directly at Luke, thanks to the hubbub of all of us getting settled in. And soon he's gone, anyway, heading out into the ocean for a swim. Meanwhile, Garrett goes off to rent a surf board, and Kenneth and Dad decide to check out some museum right off the beach. Both Catherine and Mom lay out on their beach towels and bury their noses in books. They've both got the same paperback, some brightly-covered beach read, as if they're in a book club for two.

As for me, I peel off my clothes, smear sunscreen on my onion-white skin, and lay back on my beach towel.

Without a book to keep me occupied and no one to talk to, I just soak up the sun. After a while, though, Luke comes back from swimming and sits down on the beach towel next to me, his skin still gleaming wet from the ocean. Involuntarily, I eye his taut stomach.

Why do his abs have to look like that? Why do they have to be so defined?

Luke catches me looking at him. "What?"

"Nothing," I say, averting my eyes. "How's the water?"

"It's unbelievable. You should go in."

"Maybe later."

"Well, let me know when you want to," says Luke as he lays back, resting his hands behind his head. "I'll go with you."

"Right," I say, glancing at his stomach one more time before forcing myself to stop. "Sure."

Later in the afternoon, as I'm pushing away those annoying thoughts of Luke's muscles again, Catherine informs us that we have reservations at a luau. At the announcement, Mom's eyes immediately brighten with excitement.

"Oh, Catherine," says Mom. "You thought of everything, didn't you?"

Catherine smiles, obviously pleased that she's done so well. The two of them hug.

"I just wanted this vacation to be special," says Catherine. "For everyone, I mean. But especially for you and Dad."

Shoot. I still need to get something for Mom and Dad's anniversary. Before I can forget again, I excuse myself, saying that I need to go find a bathroom.

"Public restrooms are that way," says Catherine, pointing up the beach.

"Yep," I say. I grab my wallet and break away from the group.

In the nearest gift shop, I search for something that will make a good anniversary gift. It's hard to find something, though. Everything feels so touristy. So run-of-the-mill.

Then I see it in the display case at the counter. It's so beautiful, it's almost blinding.

"Hi," I say to the girl working at the shop. "How much is that clock?"

She unlocks the case from her side, crouches down, and checks. She glances up at me. "Five hundred."

Damn it. Does *everything* cost five hundred dollars around here? I really can't afford something so expensive. But I don't see any other good options. And I'm pretty sure that Mom and Dad would love it. I can already imagine them looking at it every day—and thinking of me as they do, and—

"Ma'am?" asks the girl.

I bristle at her calling me *ma'am*. But whatever.

"I'll take it," I say.

DURING THE LUAU, we watch, entranced, as the sun goes down behind a decorated stage, as the hula dancers swirl and shake their hips, as the firelit torches lick at the night sky. The star of the night, the roasted pig, is so golden bronze that it doesn't even look real. In addition to the pig, there's also an insanely delicious buffet. And, of course, Mai Tais aplenty.

Between the entertainment, the food, and the warm, gentle breeze periodically passing through, everything feels like it's exactly how it's supposed to be. When I look across the table at Luke, it even feels like he's actually part of the family.

Luke catches me looking at him. He gives me a smile and mouths, *What?*

I subtly shake my head and lower my eyes to my plate. I stick the tines of my fork through a wedge of grilled pineapple and bring it to my mouth. *Pineapple. Focus on the pineapple. Not Luke, not his stupid beach body. Focus on the pineapple.*

A few seats down, Mom speaks up. "So, Luke. Tell us about your family. What do your parents do?"

"My mom is a bookkeeper," Luke says. "My dad teaches high school chemistry."

"How nice," Mom says. "And do you have any siblings?"

Luke shakes his head. "Nope," he says. "I'm an only child."

"I have a theory that only children turn out to be either creative geniuses or complete weirdos," says Kenneth.

Catherine knocks him in the arm. "Kenneth," she says.

"What?" says Kenneth. "I'm not calling Luke a weirdo. In fact, quite the opposite. I'm suggesting that he's a creative genius."

Luke laughs. "I don't know about that. But thanks, Kenneth. By the way, I hear that congratulations are in order. Emma told me that you two are expecting."

Catherine's face lights up. "We are," she says. "We're *so* thrilled."

"That's exciting."

"Thank you," says Catherine. "I keep telling Kenneth that we'll have to be careful not to spoil our little bean. But it's going to be awfully difficult not to. Do you want kids, Luke?"

My shoulders stiffen. I'm about to tell Luke that he doesn't have to answer Catherine's nosy question, but a waiter leans in the way to refill our water glasses.

"Sure," says Luke. "I mean, someday."

"Emma's never been the maternal sort," says Mom. "I think she even destroyed a few of her childhood dolls. Do you remember that, Emma?"

I shake my head. I bring my water glass—my now very full water glass—to my mouth. Some splashes, of course, onto my lap.

"You know, Luke," says Dad. "I've been thinking about this startup of yours."

Relief floods through me. I silently thank Dad for the change of subject.

But then Dad says, "It sounds like something that could be of use to us at the restaurant."

Great. Of course something like this would happen. Why did Luke have to pick what he did?

"Oh, that's, uh—" Luke smiles, but I can see that he's caught off guard, too. "Well, first of all, thank you."

"Could you tell me a little more about the software?" asks Dad.

I *have* to break in. "I don't think Luke wants to talk about work while he's on vacation, Dad."

"Jeez, Emma," says Catherine, scoffing. "Let them talk if they want to."

There's an awkward moment of silence. Then Dad says, "No, Emma's right. We're on vacation. Luke, we'll talk another time?"

"Sure," says Luke. "Sounds good."

After the bill comes, Mom suggests that we take a walk on the beach. We leave the luau and start to meander down the moonlit sand as a group. Slowly, though, we spread out, walking at slightly different paces as we continue on. Luke and I are the slowest ones, which is strategic on my part: as much as I can, I want to avoid being the object of scrutiny of the rest of the group.

Neither Luke nor I feel the need to talk as we walk. Not at first. We just walk, feeling the sand under our feet, watching the night surfers out in the distance. Behind us, growing softer ever so gradually as we walk away, the sound of the live music from the luau drifts.

It's Luke who breaks the silence. Glancing over at me, he says, "Can I ask you something?"

"Sure," I say.

"What's up with you and your sister?"

I look away from him. "What do you mean?"

"I mean all the tension. What's going on with you two?"

"It's always this way. We've never gotten along."

"Even when you were kids?"

"Yes. Even when we were kids. Like I said, it's always been that way."

"Have you ever said anything to her about it?" asks Luke.

"It wouldn't help."

"Maybe it would, though."

I sigh. "Why do you care so much?"

"I care because I care about you. And I thought it might help to talk about it."

"Well, I don't want to talk about it."

"Okay," he says. "That's fine."

We walk for a while further in silence. By now, we've dropped back quite a bit from the group. We're practically on our own.

I glance over at Luke. I feel bad now for snapping him.

"Hey," I say. "Thanks. It's thoughtful of you to ask."

He nods. "I know it's none of my business. I was just concerned about you. That's all."

I smirk. "Since when did you get so caring?"

"What do you mean? You're my friend. Of course I care about you."

I'm sure it's just the words, but hearing him say that he cares about me makes me feel all mushy inside. I mean, you *know* that your friends care about you, but to hear them actually say it? It feels nice.

"Well, thanks," I say.

"If you ever *do* want to talk, I'm here."

"Okay," I say. "Thank you."

I'm ready to move on to another subject. But my mind refuses to. Now I can't *not* think about how strained my relationship is with my sister. And how long it's been that way. And how sweet of a friend Luke is being. And then all at once, those feelings snowball and the tears come rushing up into my eyes. Suddenly, I'm sobbing like an idiot.

"Emma?" Luke says. "Hey, are you okay?"

He wraps his arms around me and I nod against his chest. Oh, God. What is *wrong* with me? Why do I have to embarrass myself like this?

Luke rubs my back. Then he pulls away a little. He unwraps his arms from me and lifts my chin.

"You okay?" he asks again. His face is serious and concerned.

I nod. "Yep. I just—I had a moment. That's all."

"Are you sure?"

"I'm sure. Thanks. For...comforting me."

"Of course."

"Are you regretting coming on the trip yet?" I say, smiling.

"Not at all," Luke says.

He looks like he wants to say something else, but stops.

"What?" I ask.

"Nothing," says Luke.

I'm suddenly aware of how very, very close we are standing to each other.

"No, seriously. What, Luke?" I ask. "Come on. I just broke down in front of you. The least you can do is tell me what's on your mind."

He shakes his head. I give him a forceful look.

"Tell me," I say, punching him lightly in the arm.

And that's when Luke gives me this look, this look that in a split second changes everything. And then he leans down, moves in closer, and kisses me on the lips.

The first kiss he gives me doesn't last too long. It's gentle, tentative, experimental. But when he kisses me again, our lips part; our tongues entwine. I close my eyes and sink into him. My mind is going a hundred million miles an hour. But I try to play it cool. I try to act like of *course* this was going to happen.

It's the hooting that makes us stop kissing. The hooting from my family, that is. Mortified, I pull back from Luke and wipe the saliva from my mouth. We both turn our heads to see the entirety of my family watching us.

"*Finally*," says Catherine. "I was beginning to wonder if you guys were really together."

Luke laughs nervously. I'm just glad that it's night and nobody can see how bright red my face is.

"How long have you guys been standing there?" I squeak out.

"Not long," says Mom.

"Too long, if you ask me," says Garrett.

"Oh, shut up," I say, gently.

Together, the seven of us head back down the beach. To my relief, nobody mentions the kiss again. We talk about how fantastic the luau was, how gorgeous the moon is tonight.

But my mind is elsewhere. It's still spinning. It's out of control.

Luke kissed me. Luke *kissed* me.

It's going to be an interesting night.

14

OF COURSE, though, because this is the way my life goes, after we do get back to the house and say good night to everyone, Luke and I go into our bedroom and act like nothing happened. We get ready for bed like we've done the last two nights, with me going out to use the bathroom first and then him taking his turn. And like before, I'm already in bed when he gets back. The kiss on the beach is still spinning in my mind, but as Luke silently gets into bed and stays way over on his side of the mattress, it seems as if that's all it's ever going to be.

And as far as I'm concerned, if he's not going to bring it up, neither am I. Why would I risk making any more of a fool of myself?

"Good night," I say.

"Night," Luke says. The word comes out of his

mouth clipped. Flat. Well...okay. If that's how it's going to be, that's how it's going to be.

I turn onto my side, facing away from him, shut my eyes, and wait for sleep to come. I'm not tired, though. Not at all.

Not sure what else to do, I try the old trick of counting imaginary sheep. But they just stare at me, like, *Seriously? Don't expect us to fix this, girl.*

On the other side of the bed, Luke shifts under the sheets. And then shifts again. And again. I lay there, completely still and silent, until I can't take it any longer.

"Can you stop tossing and turning?" I say.

He sighs. After a few beats, he says, "Do you want me to sleep on the floor?"

"You don't have to do that," I say. "Just stop moving around so much."

"I'm trying to get comfortable."

There's a few minutes of tense silence between us. Finally, I roll over onto my other side to face him. He's on his back, head pressed into his pillow.

"Why did you kiss me?" I ask.

He doesn't look at me. He shrugs. "It seemed like the right thing to do."

"That's not an answer."

"Well, it's my answer."

"Are you kidding me, Luke?" I say. "What does that even mean, it was the *right thing to do*?"

The words come out a lot angrier than I expect

them to. I'm not angry that he kissed me, though. It's more than I'm flabbergasted at how nonplussed he's being about it. How can this not be a big deal to him, too?

Luke grunts out a sigh. "I only did it because your family was around," he says. "I was just trying to keep this whole thing convincing."

"But they weren't around when you did it."

"They showed up eventually."

I squint at him. "You didn't know they'd come back, though."

I can see that this argument is going nowhere. But I can't let it go. Why is he being so stubborn about this?

"So you didn't mean it, then?" I ask. "It was all for show?"

"Exactly," he says.

I don't believe him. He's avoiding looking at me. And he's got this *look* on his face that I can't figure out. It's not a look I've ever seen on him before. He doesn't... he doesn't *like* me, does he? Luke doesn't have a freakin' *crush* on me, does he?

I think back to that night in his apartment, when he had a concussion. I think about how weird he started acting after I told him that I didn't like him.

"Kiss me again," I say.

His eyes finally drift over to meet mine. "What?"

"Do it again," I say. "I want you to kiss me again."

"Why?" he says.

"I need to see if I'm right," I say.

"Right about what?" he says. Annoyance has crept up into his voice. And, unless I'm totally crazy and imagining it, which I admit is a possibility, he seems a little flustered.

"I have a theory," I say. I don't want to come right out and say that I suspect he likes me, because I'm sure that will only make him defensive. And, to be honest, I'm not even sure how him kissing me again will prove anything. But it seems like the only option for us right now. It seems entirely necessary. It's the only way I'm going to figure out what's really going on here.

Luke, however, is not enthused. He just snorts a laugh and remains exactly where he is.

"Sorry," he says, shutting his eyes. "No can do."

I drop onto my back and huff out a sigh. Fine. Be difficult, then. I guess it's probably for the best, but still, I'm annoyed. He thinks he can just—

"Oh, screw it," says Luke. He rolls over in the bed toward me. And then suddenly he's right there, right up close to me, and his hand is reaching over to gently turn my face toward his.

And then he's pressing his lips to mine.

The kiss is even better than the one on the beach. And it tells me what I need to know. He *definitely* likes me. You don't fake-kiss someone like this.

Luke totally has a thing for me.

The side of his body gently brushes against mine. And I can't help it—I think about what it would be like to feel him fully press himself against me. Not that I want that to happen. That would be ludicrous. We couldn't possibly—

"Happy now?" Luke says, pulling away.

Well, *he* certainly doesn't look happy.

"That was...I..." I can't seem to find the words.

"You really want to know why I kissed you on the beach?" he says. "Emma, I kissed you because I wanted to kiss you. It's not that complicated. I like you. Okay? There. Now you can make fun of me all you want."

My heart skips a beat. Even though I suspected that he might have feelings for me, it's different actually hearing him admit it.

"Why would I make fun of you?" I ask. "I think it's...sweet."

Luke doesn't say anything. And, finally, in his silence, I get it. He thinks I'm going to pity him now. Because there's nothing sadder than a one-sided crush, now is there? It's pathetic in its own special way.

The thing is, though...I think I have feelings for him, too. I think that kiss told me more than I was expecting. I mean, when I think about it, it all seems so obvious now. Of course we've wanted each other. Of course we've been fighting back these feelings.

Of course it's why I asked him to be my fake boyfriend.

"Luke, I—"

"It's fine. You don't have to say anything." He starts to roll away. "I'll sleep on the floor."

"Luke, *stop*."

I grab his wrist, but he pulls out of my grasp. "It's fine."

"I like you, too," I blurt out.

He freezes. He turns to look at me cautiously. I watch his Adam's apple rise and fall as he swallows. And then, slowly, the doubt vanishes from his face. I don't need to say anything more. He moves toward me on the bed and kisses me again.

For the record, he's...yeah. He's a good kisser.

For several minutes, that's all we do. Kiss, I mean. And it's wonderful and gorgeous and perfect. But after a while, my hands start to get restless—and so do his. I place my hand on his chest, feeling with hazy admiration the toned muscles through his shirt. Luke's right hand moves beneath the sheets and gives my hip a squeeze. Then his hand drifts upward and his fingers reach the inch of bare skin that my shirt has ridden up and left exposed.

As his fingertips press against my skin, a little zap of electricity runs up through me. I want him. With a hundred percent certainty, I want him. Is that a surefire disaster, though? If we sleep together, things will never be the same. It's one thing for us to lock lips, another thing to...

"Hey," says Luke. "Everything okay?"

"Yeah," I say. "I just...are we going to regret this?"

"Well, let's see. Last time I checked, I couldn't see into the future. But no. I don't think we will. If you want to stop, though..."

"I don't want to stop."

"Good. Because neither do I." He pauses, then frowns. "Now that I think about it, though, this is clearly a violation of our rules."

I laugh. "I don't think we made a rule about not sleeping together."

"No? Well, that's good news."

"Very good news," I say.

"The best kind of news there is," he says.

He begins to undress me, planting kisses as he goes. I, on the other hand, do a much less elegant job of taking off his clothes. Funny, how much more difficult it is to undress someone else, when we do so much of it ourselves.

I've got a finger hooked around the waistband of Luke's boxers when he pulls my hand away and says, "Hold on." He slides out of bed and digs around in his luggage. After a minute, he triumphantly holds up a foil packet.

"Wait," I say. "You came prepared?"

"It was already in there," he says with a shrug.

"Right," I say. "That's...not convincing at all." I run through the possibilities in my head: that he was hoping we'd hook up, that he was hoping to hook up with someone *else*, that he's telling the truth and there really was a leftover condom in his luggage from some previous trip.

Am I overthinking this?

I'm definitely overthinking this.

"Look," he says. "Do you want to argue about it or do you want to use it?"

I look at him and all of his irrepressible attractiveness. I consider, with as clear of a head as I can, the possibilities that lay ahead. I see the beginning of something really special. I see a night of cringe-inducing awkwardness. But most strongly, I see my future self full of regret for not doing what my body and heart and head want.

And so I give him a look, and smooth my hands over the bed covers, and say, "I want to use it, dummy."

15

THE NEXT MORNING, when we go downstairs for breakfast, I'm convinced that everyone knows what happened last night. It's *gotta* be written all over our faces, right? It feels as obvious as if the news article that Mom is reading on her tablet is titled FAKE COUPLE SLEEPS TOGETHER AND OH MY GOD IT WAS AMAZING.

Nobody seems to notice anything, though. There's nothing more than some scattered *good mornings* as Luke and I sit down at the table. There's no snickering, no sidelong glances. So I relax—cautiously—as I shake out some cereal into a bowl. I even allow myself to sneak a glance at Luke, risking the possibility of my face flushing at the memory of the previous night.

Those worries about it being awkward? Totally unfounded. It was the complete opposite of awkward.

Luke catches me looking at him, and his mouth

instantly curls up into a smile. My heart pounds a few rapid beats. My mind goes straight to thinking about Luke's kisses, Luke's hands running over my skin. About the warmth of his body kissed against mine. I think about how nice it was to wake up this morning with those lean, strong arms of his wrapped around me—

Catherine clears her throat. I drop my eyes to my cereal bowl. Must. Not. Think. About. Last. Night. What can I think about instead? Cereal. Yes. Cereal is good.

"So," says Catherine. "We've got the portrait photographer booked this afternoon. But we have a couple different options for this morning. There's a botanical garden that I've read good things about. There's also snorkeling. Or, if you guys feel like seeing the island from *above*, I found a place that does helicopter tours."

Needless to say, when we vote, the helicopter tour beats out its competition.

You know how, every once in a while, everything feels perfect? Today is one of those times. Everyone is in a good mood. Everyone is in sync. We even somehow all end up ready to leave the house at exactly the same time.

And, as a bonus, my hair looks ridiculously good today. It *never* looks this good.

We pile into the minivan and head to our destination. The helicopters can only seat up to four people in the back, and so, when we get there, we divvy ourselves up: Garrett, Luke, and I are in the first group, and Catherine and Kenneth and our parents are in the second.

After we climb into the aircraft and get buckled in, Luke slips his hand into mine and squeezes. I still feel in sort of a state of disbelief about what's happened between us, and it's nice to get reassurance from him. *I like you*, the squeeze of his hand tells me.

I squeeze his hand back.

Luke leans over close to me. "Hey, are your parents really cool with paying for all of this? I feel like a total mooch."

I nod. "Don't worry about it. They love treating us to things like this when we're on vacation."

"Well, I'm definitely sending them a huge thank you gift after the trip."

I'm about to tell him that he really doesn't have to, but then the helicopter engine starts and suddenly I can no longer hear myself think.

Remember how I'm always convinced that the plane I'm on is going to crash? As we climb up into the air, I expect those same feelings to arise. But they don't. I don't know if it's because Luke's still holding my hand or what, but I feel utterly calm, *excited* even, to be up in the air. Below us, the island shrinks, while the gorgeous blues and aquas of the ocean expand.

It's breathtaking how much more stunning the earth looks from a thousand feet up above.

Luke and I hold hands for the duration of the ride. We even sneak in a couple of kisses—despite Garrett's protests to cut it out. When we land back where we started, I feel exhilarated. I feel completely at peace. I can't imagine a more perfect day.

After the helicopter rides, we head back to the house to eat lunch and chill out for the afternoon. When it's time to get dressed for the photographer, Luke and I get ready at the same time, taking the opportunity to spend a few minutes alone. After I change into the top that I brought for the occasion—a white sleeveless blouse, per Catherine's request—Luke takes me by the waist and pulls me into him and gives me a tender kiss.

"You look really pretty," he says.

"Aw," I say. "Thanks."

He smiles and gives me another kiss. His fingers gently graze my arm, instantly giving me goosebumps. "Think anyone would notice if we skipped the portrait session?"

I bite my lip. "Unfortunately, yes."

Five minutes later, we're all down at the beach, meeting the photographer that Catherine hired. Now, I've never really been one for getting my photo taken. It always feels so forced. In family photographs of past vacations, you can clearly see the reluctance on my face. But it's different this time. It's *fun* this time. As the portrait photographer tells us where to stand on the beach, I agreeably oblige.

The photographer takes a few photos of the whole group. Then Luke says, "Hey, I'm going to step out, okay? Since it's a family photo, I mean."

"Don't be silly, Luke," says Mom. "You're here with us. You should be in the photo."

"Yeah, we'll just edit you out if you and Emma break up," says Garrett, and everybody laughs.

We take a few more as a big group, and then some of Catherine and Garrett and me with Mom and Dad.

"Wonderful," says the photographer. "Okay. Now let's do couples, yes?"

He takes some shots of our parents first. Then he photographs Catherine and Kenneth—who, of course, do the obligatory him-standing-behind-her-cupping-her-belly shot, even though she doesn't even have one yet. Cheesy or not, though, I do have to admit that it's also sweet. As much as we don't get along, I *am* excited for my sister. I *am* excited to become an aunt.

"Okay. Next? Luke, Emma?" says the photographer, looking over his shoulder to find us.

"Oh...that's okay," I say. "I think we'll pass." Watching my parents and Catherine and Kenneth take their photos has reminded me that their relationships are real and mine isn't. Even though things feel so different now with Luke, it doesn't feel totally appropriate that he and I should take photos like this.

"What do you mean, you'll pass?" says Catherine. "Go on. Let him photograph you."

"Come on, let's do it," says Luke, slipping his hand

into mine.

It feels weird at first to be so on display in front of everyone—to pose and smile and act like it's all real. The photographer seems to sense my discomfort. He encourages me to pretend like he's not even there.

Luke must sense it, too. He gives my hand a squeeze. Then he moves his mouth a little closer to my ear.

He whispers, "The photographer's fly is down."

I see that Luke's right. I laugh.

Just then, I hear the shutter of the camera go off.

"Sorry," I say to the photographer. "Did I ruin the shot?"

"No, that's perfect!" says the photographer. He moves closer, holds up his camera again. "That's it. Good. That's beautiful. Just like that." And it's in that moment that I find myself thinking that maybe this—Luke and I—could actually work in real life. That maybe it's not so crazy after all.

THAT NIGHT, we go out to the anniversary dinner that Catherine has planned for our parents. It's a gorgeous restaurant, with the dining room low-lit and bustling, and the sound of live music floating through the room.

Luke and I are sitting next to each other, but we're engaged in two different conversations. I'm talking to

Garrett about school, asking him about his courses and plans for the rest of the summer. Meanwhile, Luke is talking to Dad about his supposed startup.

Ugh. The startup.

Ever since Dad showed a little too much interest in Luke's business, I've worried that the lie would be our undoing. But as I continue to eavesdrop on their conversation, I'm relieved to hear Luke answer Dad's questions with ease—and then, without faltering, giving him a totally plausible reason for why his marketing software might not be the best fit for Dad's business needs.

Luke does it with such tact, such effortlessness, that I can't help but feel impressed. But the longer I sit there, the more the feeling morphs into guilt. I hate that he has to lie to Dad like this. This wasn't what I imagined when I asked Luke to pretend that he was an entrepreneur. I thought it would be simpler, less involved. Call me naive, but I thought it would impress my parents, then never be mentioned again.

There's something else nagging at me, too, though. It's not only guilt I feel. I'm unsettled. Luke is *so* good at pulling the wool over someone's eyes.

What if he's doing that to me, too?

No. I need to stop psyching myself out. Luke wouldn't do something like that. Besides, the fibs he's telling Dad are ones I *asked* him to tell. Not in so much detail, but still. He's doing what he needs to do.

My thoughts are interrupted by Catherine asking

for everyone's attention. She stands up from her chair and raises her virgin piña colada up into the air.

"To Mom and Dad," says Catherine. "The best role models a girl could have ever asked for. Happy early thirtieth anniversary, you two. I love you guys."

We all give a little cheer and clink glasses. After we drink, Catherine holds out an envelope to Mom, who opens it and then says, "Oh, honey. You didn't need to get us anything."

"We wanted to," says Catherine, threading her arm through Kenneth's.

Mom shows off the contents of the envelope to the rest of us: it's a gift card for a spa.

"It's a local place," says Catherine. "There's enough on there for a couple's massage."

"That sounds lovely," says Mom. "Is this the same spa that you and Luke went to, Emma?"

Without even looking at her, I can feel Catherine's glare trained on me.

"Um," I say. "I think it's a different one." I reach down and pull the gift I bought for my parents out of my bag. It's been beautifully wrapped, courtesy of the shop I bought it from.

"I have something for you, too," I say. "Happy anniversary, Mom and Dad."

"*Another* gift?" says Mom. She shakes her head, but accepts it from me. She carefully undoes the bow and removes the paper. "Oh. Goodness. This is...this is gorgeous, Emma."

"Look at that detail work," says Dad, leaning in to get a better look.

"I'm glad you like it," I say, my chest warming.

Later, though, after we get home, Mom pulls me aside. She's holding the box that the clock came in, the gift paper still half-wrapped around it.

I look at her questioningly, worried that there's something wrong with the clock. She returns my gaze with a careful look.

"It was very nice of you to give us this gift, Emma," she says. "But we can't accept it."

I feel a little sick. "What do you mean, you can't accept it?"

"It's too much. You shouldn't have spent so much on something for us."

"It's for your anniversary."

"And we appreciate the gesture. Very much so. But you should return it. Save the money."

She presses the box into my hands. I have no choice but to take it back from her. Embarrassed, I carry it up to my room. Before Luke can see what I'm doing, I shove it into my luggage.

"Hey," Luke says, looking up from his phone. "There you are."

I smile at him, pushing away my pain. "What, have you been waiting for me or something?"

"Guilty as charged," he says. He sets his phone aside and waves me over to the bed. "Come 'ere, Armstrong. You look like you need a massage."

16

THE NEXT MORNING, while Mom and Dad are out at the spa, I decide to plan a little something for Luke and I to do on our own. Half an hour of internet sleuthing later, I find the perfect thing. If I'm going to succeed in pulling it off, though, we'll have to leave right away.

I hurry downstairs and find Luke in the living room playing a board game with Kenneth.

"Hey," I say. "You guys almost done?"

"Not really," Luke says, moving a piece on the board.

"Can I persuade you to put your game on pause, then?"

"Why?" he asks.

"It's a surprise."

"What kind of surprise?"

I sigh. "Seriously?"

"Okay, okay," says Luke, pulling himself up. "To be continued, Kenneth?"

"To be continued," agrees Kenneth. He holds up his palm. "I solemnly swear to not make any moves while you're gone."

Since Mom and Dad have the minivan, I call us a cab. When it shows up, I run outside and tell the driver where we're headed, then ask him to not mention our destination while we're driving. Then I run back inside, yell out to Luke that the cab's here, and wait impatiently for him to join me.

"Jeez," says Luke. "What's the huge rush?"

"Less talking, more walking," I say, tugging his arm. "Come *on*."

When we get into the cab, the driver winks at me ridiculously in the rear view mirror, then brings us to our destination: a beach on the west side of the island. When we get out, Luke gives me a look that says, *This is it? A beach?* But when we walk further, going down a small path that spits out into a more secluded area, the real star attraction becomes evident. There, scattered across the beach, are tons of beautiful sea turtles.

"Whoa," says Luke.

"I know," I say. "Right?"

Luke grins at me. "How'd you find out about this place?"

"Oh, you know. A little thing called the internet."

"There goes one," he says. We watch as one of the

turtles disappears into the ocean. "We aren't scaring them off, are we?"

"No. They only hang out on the beach certain times of day."

"Ah," says Luke. "Okay. Now all the rushing to get here makes sense."

"Well, yeah," I say. "What, you think I'd act that crazy for no reason?"

Luke shrugs, and I punch him playfully in the shoulder.

As the rest of the turtles gradually leave, Luke and I sit on a large flat rock nearby and watch them go. It's a nice moment to share. It's actually pretty romantic. I lean my head on his shoulder and thread my fingers through his. He rubs the pad of his thumb over my skin, the kind of touch that spreads warmth through my whole body.

A few minutes later, the peaceful silence is ruined by the chime of Luke's cell phone. I keep my head on his shoulder, though, as he uses his free hand to dig his phone out of his pocket.

"Anything important?" I ask.

"Nah," he says.

His phone chimes again.

"Um, not to be that annoying person," I say. "But would you mind muting your phone?"

Less than a minute later, there's another chime. I lift my head off his shoulder.

"Some of the rugby guys are texting," says Luke, swiping his screen. "Sorry."

"Just put your phone on silent."

"I thought I did."

"Well, obviously, you didn't."

Luke screws up his face. "Don't get so upset. It was a mistake."

His phone doesn't chime again after that. But I continue to feel irritated. The outing feels ruined.

I try to concentrate on the turtles. There's only a few left on the beach now. In silence, Luke and I watch the remaining ones slowly make their way to the water.

"Hey," says Luke, nudging me gently. "Thanks for bringing me out here."

I shrug. "I mean, I know it's no helicopter ride."

"Are you kidding? This is just as cool."

"Well, I'm glad we caught them," I say.

"Me, too," he says. "Hey, are we all good?"

I look at him. I can't resist his earnest eyes. I nod. "Yeah. We're good."

A speck of water lands on my nose, and then another on my cheek. It's beginning to rain. Within minutes, the light sprinkle grows to a constant fall of fat little raindrops.

We call for a cab, but I can already tell that unless one is super close by, we're going to be soaked by the time it picks us up. Then I remember the compact umbrella that Paige lent me. I dig through my bag and pull it out. With one click, the tiny thing expands above our heads.

"Look at you," says Luke.

"It's Paige's, actually," I say. "I thought she was nuts for lending it to me, but...well...here we are."

"Here we are," says Luke, and kisses me as the raindrops drum overhead.

"SO, EMMA," says Catherine. "Tell us more about you and Luke."

It's later in the day and I'm on the back patio at the house with Mom and Catherine. The guys are all doing other things—Luke and Kenneth have resumed their board game, Dad is taking a nap, and Garrett is on his phone.

"What do you want to know?" I ask.

Catherine sips her iced tea. She has flame red lipstick on today. "How serious are you guys?"

I hesitate. I think about my conversation with Luke back at the airport, when we agreed that when it came to our fake relationship, we were in love. But it feels too weird to say now that real feelings are involved.

"We're pretty serious," I say.

"And you've been seeing each other for how long again?" asks Catherine.

"Um...I mean, it's only been a few weeks. But it feels like it's been a lot longer than that."

"Wow," says Catherine, disapprovingly. "Serious so soon. I know you haven't have a boyfriend in a long time, so you're probably falling for this guy extra hard. But be careful."

"I'm fine, thanks," I say.

"It's good that you're dating, Emma," says Mom. "You should have all the fun you can."

"Right, but...you like Luke, don't you, Mom?"

"I do," she says. "Catherine's right, though. There's no reason to rush things."

"I'm not trying to rush things," I say. "It's just how it is."

Mom examines her arm. "Would you mind passing me the sunscreen, Emma?"

I grab the bottle. "Hold out your arm. I'll squeeze some out."

She does as I suggest. But when I squeeze the bottle, I accidentally cover her arm in a huge glob.

"Sorry," I say. "Jeez. Here, let me—"

I try to suck some of it back into the bottle, but more comes out.

"It's fine," says Mom.

"You know," says Catherine, "one of Kenneth's coworkers recently moved up north."

"Um, okay," I say. I snap the cap back on the sunscreen and toss it aside.

"The two of you should meet," says Catherine.

"What? Why? I'm in a relationship."

"Yeah, but you've only been seeing Luke for a few weeks."

I exhale. I should have expected this. Even when I bring a boyfriend on vacation, they *still* find a way to dismiss it. "Can we talk about something else?"

"Of course," says Mom. She's finally finished rubbing the sunscreen into her arm. "How's work going?"

"It's fine," I say.

"Nothing new?" asks Mom.

I don't really want to talk about it, but I don't want the conversation to return to my love life, either. "Well...there might be a managerial position opening up."

"That's a big role to step into, being a manager," says Catherine.

"Yeah," I say stiffly. "I know."

"I know the raise probably seems appealing, but it would be a lot of—"

"Could you stop?" I snap.

Nobody says anything for a few seconds.

Then Catherine says, "Excuse me?"

Part of me wants to get up and leave. To walk away from this conversation. To flee. But the part of me that's fed up is more determined. I've finally had enough.

I look my sister in the eye and say, "Stop treating me like a child. Stop picking apart everything about my life."

"What are you talking about?" says Catherine.

"Oh, come on. You just did it. You just dismissed my relationship with Luke. And you act like I don't realize that a promotion would mean more responsibility. Just because you're older, and married, and you're out saving the planet every day, you think you're entitled to talk to me like that, but—"

"It's not about feeling *entitled*," says Catherine. "I'm looking out for you."

"Well, I don't need looking out for."

"Okay, then," says Catherine. She rolls her eyes. "I'll keep that in mind for the future."

"Girls," says Mom. "Please. Let's calm down."

"You know," says Catherine, ignoring Mom, "if you acted more mindfully, Emma, I wouldn't feel the need to say anything."

I laugh dryly. "Right."

"You're always late when we have a family Skype call. And you invited a guy you've only known for a few *weeks* along on our vacation without even *asking* if the rest of us were cool with it. But you know what really irks me? You couldn't even be bothered to help me plan this trip."

"Are you serious?" I say. "You didn't give me a chance to."

"I texted you *numerous* times!"

"Yeah, after you'd already done the research or booked things."

"You could have done it, too, Emma," says Catherine. "You could have taken the initiative."

"And step on your toes? No thanks. Then you would have just been upset about *that*."

"No. Not true."

"Admit it," I say. "No matter what I do, you'll find something wrong with it. It's always been that way. You're perfect, and I'm flawed. Well, you don't have to constantly remind me of it. Trust me, I'm well aware. As are Mom and Dad."

Catherine frowns. She opens her mouth, then closes it. Mom shakes her head.

"Honey," says Mom. "Nobody's perfect."

"Some people sure act like they are," I say.

Behind us, the door to the patio slides open.

"Iced tea incoming," says Kenneth, carrying a large pitcher. He refills our glasses as we sit in silence. "Can I bring you ladies anything else?"

"We're fine," says Catherine.

"Thank you, Kenneth," says Mom. "But I think it's about time we head inside and cool off, anyway."

17

I SIT AS FAR AWAY AS possible from Catherine that night at dinner—which, along with some mahi-mahi that Mom runs out to get from the store, consists of eating up the hodgepodge of food we've picked up over the last several days. After we finish eating, I help clean up the dishes, then head upstairs to go to bed. I'm not exactly in the mood to socialize anymore, and our flight is early the next morning.

I'm almost to the bedroom when I hear Catherine say my name. I turn around and see her coming up the stairs behind me.

"Hey, Emma?" she says tentatively. "Can I talk to you for a second?"

My body tenses. I really don't want to get into a fight with her again.

"What is it?" I say.

"About earlier...I guess I didn't realize how harsh I've been."

"I find that hard to believe," I say.

"Well, whether or not you believe it, it's true. And I'm sorry. I'm going to try to change."

Our eyes meet. She looks sincere. But it's hard to let everything go just like that.

"I appreciate you saying that, Catherine, but...I mean, actions speak louder than words."

Catherine nods. "Fair enough."

Silence hangs between us.

"Look, I won't bring it up again after this. But *please*, Emma, be careful with Luke. You don't know him very well. I don't want you to do something you'll regret."

"You don't have to worry about that," I say.

"I do, though, Emma. Because it's happened to me. I don't think I ever told you about this, but there was this guy I dated before I met Kenneth, someone I fell for really fast. We even talked about getting married, which was absolutely crazy in hindsight. Let's just say that he didn't end up being as trustworthy as I thought. And I don't want you to make the type of mistake that I almost did."

I wish right then that I could explain everything to Catherine. That I could tell her the whole truth. But I can't, and I don't. I just nod.

"Like I said, I'm going to try to change," says Catherine.

"Okay," I say. "Thanks."

"Well, goodnight."

"Goodnight," I say.

With softened feelings, I watch her head back downstairs.

In our bedroom, I find Luke lying on top of the covers, scrolling through his phone. He glances over at me and smiles. Ugh. That smile. How is he so attractive all the time?

"I've got some good memes to show you," he says.

"Yeah?" I say. "Good. I need a laugh." I haven't told him about my argument with Catherine, but I don't feel like getting into it yet. All I want to do right now is relax.

I settle into bed beside him, snuggling up against his shoulder. Luke holds the phone so that both of us have a good view of the screen. As he scrolls through the memes—of cats and crazed kids and celebrities—we laugh at the best ones. I'm touched that he knows exactly what I need.

Luke is scrolling down again when a notification pops up on his screen. *Hey, hottie! You've received a new Heartthrob message! Swipe to read.*

Almost instantly, Luke dismisses the notification.

"Uh," I say. "What was that?"

"Nothing," he says.

My heart lurches in my chest. "Was that from a dating app?"

"I mean, yeah. But it's nothing."

I think back to this morning on the beach, when his phone kept going off. I think of all the other times he's been on it, too, this trip. I feel like such a fool.

I sit up in bed and look at him.

"You've been using it this whole time," I say.

"I mean, if someone messages me, I'm going to reply. What's the big deal?"

I stare at him in disbelief. Does he really not understand why I would care? This is no longer just some stupid arrangement. This is…okay, I don't know what it is. But I do know that I hate the fact that he's been messaging other women.

"Hey, come on," says Luke, setting down his phone, "we never said that using a dating app was off-limits. We only agreed that we wouldn't go out on any dates with anyone else. Remember?"

"We slept together," I say.

"We did," Luke says slowly. "But…you don't think we're in a real relationship now, do you?"

"No," I say. "But, Luke, things have changed. You can't deny that."

"I'm not denying it. But this isn't a real relationship. And so you can't get pissed at me for using some stupid dating app."

"You were getting messages when we were at the beach. You were looking at them."

"What? No. I told you, those were texts from the rugby guys." He picks his phone up and unlocks the screen. "Here, you want to read the texts?"

"No."

"Because you can. I don't care. I'll even show you the dating app."

"Stop. I don't want to see it."

"I'm not trying to hide anything from you, Emma."

I lean back against the headboard. I don't say anything for a while. I'm both frustrated with him and frustrated with myself. Most of all, I'm frustrated with this gray area that we've found ourselves in. "So, what, we sleep together in Hawaii and that's it? After we get home, we're going to pretend like it never happened?"

"Whoa. I never said that."

"That's what you're acting like, though."

"You're reading too much into things."

"Well then *talk* to me, Luke. Because it's pretty frustrating to try to guess how you're feeling."

"Look," says Luke. "I've had a lot of fun with you here. But I honestly haven't thought about what's going to happen when we get back home. I really haven't."

More silence passes. Outside, a light breeze whispers through the palm trees.

Luke shifts in the bed. He smiles cautiously. I guess he's trying to lighten the mood. "Are you in love with me or something, Armstrong?"

"Um, no?" I say.

"You sure? Because I wasn't going to say anything. But I've seen the way you always sneak glances at me at work."

"*Sneak glances* at you? I don't sneak glances at you."

"Deny it all you want, but I've seen it. I've seen the way you look at me."

I don't have a clue what he's talking about. But it takes me only a few seconds to realize his mistake. "*Oh.* Um, no, Luke. Sorry to burst your bubble, but it's not you I've been looking at. It's Alex."

"Alex?" says Luke. The smile drops off his face. "Alex...Clarke?"

"What other Alex is there?" I say. "Yes. Alex Clarke."

"Oh." Luke rubs the back of his neck. "So, you're in love with *him*?"

"What? No. Why would you think that?"

"Like I said. All the lovelorn looks at work."

I roll my eyes. "Now you're the one reading too much into things."

"I'm just saying what I saw."

"Well, to put the record straight, I'm not in love with him. I'm not in love with anyone. Not even close."

"Okay. Got it."

"Especially not you," I say.

It's not that I intend to say something so hurtful. It just comes out. It's so stupid, but in that moment, it feels necessary to say something so awful in order to not get my own feelings hurt.

"Wow," says Luke. "Okay. Well...glad you got that off your chest."

I feel like crying. I feel like ripping something up. But all I can do is sit there in silence, and Luke does the same. Eventually, I get out of bed, grab my sleeping clothes, and leave to go change and brush my teeth. By the time I get back, Luke is asleep, turned toward the other side of the bed.

IN THE MORNING, knowing that we're all going to be fighting for the bathroom before we leave, I get up before everyone else to take a shower. I grab a change of clothes from my bag, quietly pad down the hall to the bathroom, and hang my bath towel near the shower before stepping in. After the argument last night with Luke, the hot water feels extra therapeutic on my skin. I vigorously knead shampoo into my hair and slather my body with soap.

I'm just about to rinse out the shampoo when the water temperature fluctuates, shifting from lusciously warm to painfully hot. Grimacing, I reach out to adjust the shower handle. But it doesn't budge. I tug it harder, stepping out of the too-hot stream of the shower. The stupid handle is still stuck. Using both hands this time, I grunt and pull on the handle again.

With a terrible crack, the handle comes flying off in my hands.

In disbelief, I stare at the piece of broken hardware. I try to put it back on, but it's pointless, of course. The shower is still running, and is still as hot as ever. Clumps of shampoo suds drip onto my shoulders.

I take a deep breath, then duck my head under the stream and rinse out my hair faster than I've ever rinsed it before. Then, frantically, I get out of the still-running shower, get speed-dressed, and rush back to the bedroom.

Luke groans when I shake him awake.

"What *is* it?" he says, his eyes still shut.

"*Look*," I say, and he opens his eyes just enough to see the dripping handle in my hands.

Back in the bathroom, Luke tries to shut off the water, but he can't do it, either.

"I think we need to turn the water off," he says.

"Yeah, no kidding, Sherlock," I say.

Luke looks unamused. "I meant the water supply to the house."

"Well, do you know where it is?"

"No. Do you?"

I sigh. "Why would I ask *you* if I knew where it was?"

Out in the hallway, footsteps approach. Then I hear Dad's voice saying, "Is everything okay?"

I look at Luke, sigh, and grab the handle from him.

"Dad," I say, stepping out of the steam-congested bathroom, "we need your help."

THE GOOD NEWS is that we figure out where the main water shut-off valve is. The bad news is that the shower is broken beyond what any of us can repair. I apologize profusely to my parents for breaking it, and assure them that I'll pay whatever the owner of the rental charges them for it.

"Don't worry about it, Emma," Dad says.

"It was an accident," Mom says.

Still, I can see the exasperation and disappointment in their eyes. It's not like I blame them, either. I've done nothing but cause problems while we've been here.

For the next few hours, while we're still in the presence of my family, Luke and I pretend that everything's okay between the two of us. Over breakfast, Luke tells them how great of a time he had. He even jokes about looking forward to the next trip. But as soon as we part ways from them, a bitterly cold silence resumes between us. When I tell Luke I need to make a pitstop on our way to the airport to return the clock, his response is a monotone, "Fine."

At the airport, as we wait for our plane to board, I dread the upcoming hours sitting next to him.

In the end, though, we don't end up sitting next to each other on the flight, because Luke switches seats with a girl to let her sit closer to her family. I can't say I'm not relieved. A part of me is disappointed, though. It's not like I expected us to work things out during the flight, but...well, there was always a chance.

For the next five hours, I do everything I can to keep my mind off of Luke. I stare out the window at the ever-changing clouds. I take an uncomfortable nap. I sip my ginger ale and nibble on my complimentary nuts. After a while, though, I can't help it. My eyes drift. I look at the back of Luke's head a few rows ahead of me. It's a view I'm so familiar with—it's the view, more or less, that I have of him every day at work. But there's something so different about it now.

So much for the brilliance of us faking a relationship.

And what was it all for? I'm no better off than I was before the trip. In fact, Mom and Dad are even less impressed with me now. Sure, *maybe* Catherine's going to start being nicer to me. But I'll believe it when I see it.

And as far as things with Luke go, well, I've clearly screwed everything up.

Emma Armstrong, world-class moron at your service.

18

IT DOESN'T FEEL like there's much of anything to be grateful for after coming back from Hawaii. I am, however, grateful for having a wide-open weekend to wallow. And wallow I do. I put on my most comfortable, ugliest lounge clothes and don't change out of them for two days. I order copious amounts of Chinese food. I finish off the two pints of ice cream in my freezer, first scraping off the ice crystals glimmering on the surface. I become one with the couch and let the saturated glow of the television pacify my mind.

But it's not until Sunday night, when I finally peel myself up and force myself to take a shower, that I finally break down. I guess there's something about the water, and its unrelenting insistence, that finally gets my tears going.

* * *

MONDAY MORNING, when I show up to work, I'm greeted by Lucinda's expectant face and an inquiry into how our vacation was.

"Hawaii was beautiful," I say. I lower my voice and drop my eyes. "Just so you know, though, Luke and I broke up."

"What?" says Lucinda. "Emma, for real? God. I'm so sorry."

I nod my thanks. I swallow down the sour knot in my throat.

"How are you holding up?" Lucinda asks, gently touching my arm.

Behind us, the elevator doors emit a metallic groan as they open. I know without looking that Luke is walking out of them. My suspicions are confirmed as Lucinda gives me a protective squeeze on the arm and says, flatly, "Hello, Luke. Welcome back."

"Hi Lucinda," says Luke, and walks past us without saying anything more.

"Oh, how *awful* for you," says Lucinda, rubbing my arm. The sadness in her eyes is almost unbearable.

I gather myself up. "We realized that we're better off as friends," I say, reciting the break up story that Luke and I agreed on when this whole stupid thing started. At the time, I felt clever, because it meant we'd be able to go right back to the way things were pre-fake-relationship. But now I know our friendship will never be what it was.

"What a disappointment!" says Lucinda. "You two made such a cute couple."

"Well," I say, shrugging.

"If you need someone to talk to, I'm here, of course. *Any* time."

I tell her I appreciate it.

Lucinda, of course, spreads the news around the office. And I'm glad that she does. Thanks to her, I have far fewer awkward conversations that day. When people ask me how Hawaii was, we talk about it as if Luke was never part of the equation.

As much as I want to block out Luke that day, though, I do have to keep tabs on him. I really don't want to bump into him around the office. So any time I have to get up from my desk, I first check to make sure he's still at his, and if he's not, I wait until he returns before getting up myself.

Mostly, it isn't hard to do. But then lunchtime rolls around. And I don't know what kind of gargantuan lunch Luke eats that day, or if he goes for a three-mile-post-lunch walk or what, but it's nearly two o'clock by the time he oh-so casually returns to his desk. I glare at the back of his head and get up from my desk to head to the break room, stomach growling. When I get there, it's totally empty, of course. I yank my lunch sack out of the refrigerator and plop down at one of the tables.

I'm almost done eating my sandwich when Alex walks in, coffee mug in hand. He doesn't say anything to me when he comes in, or as he refills his cup with fresh coffee, but when he's done, he looks over at me and nods.

"Hey," he says.

"Hey," I say back, trying to sound chill. I quickly swipe the sides of my mouth to check for crumbs. "How's it going?"

And who knows if it's because Alex has heard about the break up and feels sorry for me, or it's because I'm the only one in the break room, or it's just because he feels like doing so, but he stays. He leans against the counter, sips his coffee, and stays.

We talk about Hawaii. He tells me about a fond childhood memory he has of going there. We agree that freshly cracked-open coconuts are pretty much the best thing ever. I ask if he has any vacations coming up himself, and he tells me about the places he'd like to go. It's ordinary small talk, but it's the kind of ordinary small talk my old self would have killed to have with him.

And yet. Now that we're having it, now that Hawaii has happened with Luke, it doesn't have any effect on me. There are no butterflies. There are no shivery feelings of longing. It's as plain as day: I don't have a crush on Alex anymore.

And maybe, all along, I was lying to myself anyway.

Maybe I really was staring at Luke after all.

When I get back to my desk, I let work swallow me up. I keep my head down, stay focused, and get as much done as I can. It's not until half past six that I look up and realize how late it is. Blinking away the bleariness that comes with working for hours on end, I look around and see that there are only a few other people still at the office, and they're packing up.

Luke, thankfully, is already gone.

By seven, I'm the only one left in the office. By seven forty-five, I've caught up on everything I wanted to catch up on. Most importantly, I've finished a report that I told Sherrie I'd have done by the end of the day. In addition to that, the number of vendor applications sitting in the queue are at an all-time low. I toy with the idea of staying even later and getting through the rest of them—I've never gotten the folder down to zero, and I kind of believe that if I ever do, a magical elf or something will appear—but I'm dead tired. If I keep working, I might make a mistake. I need to call it a night.

I close the vendor applications folder, print off the report for Sherrie, and swing by the printer on my way to her office. Sherrie's door is ajar, and I let myself in to set the report on her desk.

Her desk is a mess, though, with papers scattered everywhere. I worry about my report getting lost. Should I wait until the morning to give it to her? Maybe it's better to hand it over in person, anyway? I consider it, but I like the idea of Sherrie seeing my report first thing in the morning. I set the report on her desk, front and center, making it as obvious as possible. And then, to make it even more obvious, I push a few of the other papers out of the way.

Now, for the record, I don't mean to look at any of the other papers on her desk. It just kind of happens. It's like when there's a dead animal on the side of the road and your eyes snap right to it, no matter how much you'd prefer them not to. And in this case, the lump of roadkill that my eyes snap to is a sheet of paper with a list of employee names. Not just a list of employee names, though. A list of employee names with indecipherable marks beside them.

Staring at the list, I get a nagging feeling in my gut.

This can't be good. This *can't* be good.

Just then, there's a noise outside the room. I jerk away from her desk and try to act as naturally as possible. As I walk out of Sherrie's office, I brace myself, preparing myself to see her—preparing myself to be confronted about why I was snooping around.

But it's not Sherrie, of course. It's the night janitor. He's wheeling his cart through the office, grabbing trash cans from beneath desks and emptying them out. When he sees me, he gives me a friendly nod.

"Have a good night," I call out, and rush to leave.

All the way home, I debate with myself about what I saw. If it is what I'm afraid it is, I've *got* to warn Luke. Just because we're not talking to each other right now, that doesn't mean that I'm not going to look out for him when it comes to something like this.

That night, after chewing on it for a while longer, I decide to send two texts.

The first is to Luke. *Just so you know, I saw something on Sherrie's desk, and I think there might be layoffs coming.*

Ten minutes later, my phone chimes. *Thx for the heads up.*

Next, I text Lucinda the same thing.

She texts back right away. *Emma, thank you for telling me. I'm in disbelief!*

I think back to our group bowling date, when Lucinda shared the rumor with us that Sherrie was leaving. I guess she got it wrong, though. It's some of us who are leaving soon.

I wish I'd had more time to study the list when I was in Sherrie's office. I wish I'd been thinking straight enough to take a picture of the list with my phone. Not that it would have necessarily helped. Even with a photo, I'd probably still be sitting here just as clueless as I am without one.

Here's one thing I do know, though: I'm not going to be caught unprepared.

I grab my laptop, pull up my resume, and get it up to date. Then I spend the rest of the night applying to jobs. The only part of each application that gives me pause is the section asking for references. Each time, I put down Luke's name and contact info. Then delete it. Then put it back again.

19

WHEN I GET into work the next morning, I'm on high alert, anticipating the announcement of the inevitable doomed staff meeting. But hours pass and nothing happens. Finally, unable to take it any longer, I do my best casual walk over to Sherrie's office. She's sitting nonchalantly at her desk as if everything's perfect normal.

I draw in a breath and rap gently on her door frame. Sherrie looks up from her computer screen and smiles.

"Emma," she says. "Come on in! How was Hawaii? I haven't gotten a chance to ask you about it yet."

"It was good, thanks," I say. I take an awkward step into her office. "But I actually came by because I wanted to touch base with you. I left a report on your desk last night—you got it, right?"

"I did," says Sherrie. "Thanks for putting in those extra hours. It doesn't go unnoticed." She smiles at me again. This time, though, the smile seems a little off—like maybe she just realized that I saw the layoff list on her desk.

What is *wrong* with me? Why did I have to say anything about the report?

"I love your blouse, by the way," I say.

"Oh?" says Sherrie, glancing down. She's wearing a mustard yellow top with frills for sleeves. I don't know why I said I loved it. It's pretty hideous, to tell you the truth. I really should keep my mouth shut for the rest of the day.

"You know, it's funny," says Sherrie. "I'd actually thrown this in my donate pile a couple weeks ago. But it caught my eye again this morning, so I figured I'd give it one more shot."

"You should keep it," I say.

"You think?" she says. She brushes something off her sleeve.

"Oh, definitely," I say.

"Well," says Sherrie. "I'll keep your suggestion in mind."

There's no staff meeting called that day. Nor the next. But I do hear back from one of the jobs I applied to, and we make arrangements to do a phone interview the following day. And that's when I remember the references I listed on my application, and realize that I completely forgot to give any of them a heads up.

Immediately, I message Luke. We haven't messaged each other since before our trip, and the last lines of conversation in the chat window are about what time we should schedule our Uber for.

Hey, I type. *FYI, I listed you as a reference on a job application. Hope that's ok.*

Luke replies, *Jumping ship already, huh?*

Just preparing for the worst.

When Luke doesn't say anything in response, I minimize the window. Then I open it back up and type, *You aren't looking for a plan b?*

I don't know yet, Luke types. *Gonna wait and see.*

The following day, I consume my homemade cheese sandwich like it's the antidote to all my problems and then duck into the stairwell to take the phone interview. Despite my nerves, the distracting echo of the stairwell, and the smidgen of cheddar lodged in my back molar, the interview goes well.

Really well, actually. I kind of *rock* it.

But as I get back to work, I gradually become overwhelmed with emotions of the worst sort. I feel guilty for doing the interview, anxious about the impending layoffs, and still just as crestfallen about the whole mess with Luke. I lift my face to look at him—to look at the back of his head, that is. At the stupid, handsome back of his head. I wish so badly that he would turn and look at me. That he would give me a smile. But he doesn't, of course. And something tells me that he's not going to for a long time.

* * *

THERE'S MORE traffic than usual when I drive to Dance Den that evening, and by the time I arrive, everyone is already in the studio. I quickly pay. I sign in. I rush into the bathroom to change. A flurry of clothing and elbow-smacks-against-the-bathroom-stall later, I emerge and hustle into the studio. As usual, Carla is at the front of the room guiding the group through the warmup, encouraging everyone to go deeper into their knee bends.

We're finishing up the stretches when I see a familiar face in the crowd. I have to do a double take, thinking my mind is playing tricks on me. But no. It really is her. I'm not imagining things.

Paige sees me and grins and waves.

Look, I know I don't own the place. I know that Paige has every right to be here, just as much as anyone does. Still, I can't help but feel like a sacred space of mine has been encroached upon. And it's not a good feeling. Not good at all.

As the music starts, as the dancing begins, I try to shut Paige out of my mind. I try to concentrate solely on the rhythm of the music. But no matter how hard I try, she's still there. And then I realize that she's getting *closer* to me. She has gradually been making her way across the room.

By the end of the current song, she has sidled her way right up next to me.

"Hi, Emma!" she shouts over the opening beats of

the next song. "This place is *great*! Do you know if they sell punch cards?"

Well, that's that. Dance Den is ruined. At least it was good while it lasted.

I shake my head at Paige's question. Paige shouts back, "Huh! They should!" Meanwhile, up front, Carla calls out instructions to join hands with our neighbor. I glance to my left, away from Paige, but the woman on that side of me has already paired up with someone else. Reluctantly, I turn back in the other direction.

Paige's hands are extended to receive mine.

The first unexpected thought I have while I dance with Paige is that her hands are impressively soft. She must use hand cream like nobody's business. Maybe she even uses those creepy moisturizing gloves.

But the second, and more surprising, unexpected thought I have is that, lo and behold, she's actually *fun* to dance with. She's relaxed and confident. She teaches me some of her moves. And as we dance, as the music swells around us, something absolutely preposterous happens.

It feels like we're actually friends.

A little over an hour later, class is over. In the crowded lobby, I lose sight of Paige. But as I make my way outside, I hear her calling out my name. For once, the sound of her voice doesn't make me cringe.

I turn around and watch as she materializes from the crowd.

"What a blast!" she says.

"I know, right?" I say. And I smile at her. Just a regular, genuine smile. I can't explain it, but I no longer feel annoyed by her. Maybe the magic of Dance Den has something to do with it. Maybe it's finally hit me that despite her weirdness, she's actually pretty nice. In any case, whatever it is, things are suddenly different between us now.

I ask her if she wants to grab a smoothie.

"Absolutely," she says.

AT THE SMOOTHIE BAR, Paige and I sit on the upholstered stools that look out the front window. We watch as other people from Dance Den wander by. A lot of them are in pairs or small groups, their faces brightly lit up as they chitchat with each other.

I glance over at Paige, unsure of what kind of small talk to make. It's been a long time since I've made a new friend.

"How's your smoothie?" I ask.

"Not bad," she says. She holds her cup out to me. "Wanna try?"

"Oh, that's...no, that's okay. Thanks, though."

She shrugs, then lowers her mouth and takes an extremely long drink, noisily sucking up the smoothie through her straw.

"Oh, by the way," I say. "I need to give you back your mini umbrella. Thanks for lending it to me. We did end up using it after all."

"I thought you might," she says. She frowns at me. "I heard you and Luke broke up."

I nod. "We did."

"Not-so-fun fact," says Paige. "Flamingo relationships split up ninety-nine percent of the time."

Okay. I guess she is still a little irritating.

"How do you know stuff like that?" I ask.

Paige shrugs. "It's out there."

"Right," I say. "Well...as far as Luke and I are concerned, we never should have started dating in the first place. It was a huge mistake."

"No, it wasn't."

I raise my eyebrows and wait for her to go on.

"You've learned something from it," she says. "So you're better off than you were before."

I laugh through my nose. "Sorry. But I'm pretty sure I'm *worse* off than before. I completely screwed up my friendship with Luke."

"You'll repair it."

She sounds so confident that for a second, I almost feel convinced of it, too. "I don't know. It doesn't feel very fixable."

"Why not?"

"Because..." I sigh. "Things have changed. Permanently, I think."

"You fell in love with him."

"No," I stammer. "I didn't—"

"Lemme guess. You admitted your feelings, but he didn't reciprocate them? Is that what happened?"

"No," I say forcefully. "That's not what happened. Can we please talk about something else?"

Paige scratches her arm. "Like?"

"Like..." I scramble for something, anything. "Have you cooked anything new lately?"

Sure enough, as soon as I bring up the topic, Paige is more than happy to talk about it. Relief washes over me as she starts telling me about the latest recipe she's been developing—a concoction that features macerated blueberries and tuna fish. I listen to her, but at the same time, her verdict about my breakup with Luke keeps echoing through my mind. In love with him? No. I think I'd know if *that* had happened. You don't fall in love with someone and not realize it. Sure, I developed a crush on him. But that was it. If it was anything more—

But the more I try to deny it, the more obvious it becomes.

I totally fell in love with Luke.

20

THE NEXT MORNING, shortly after I get to work, an email pops up in my inbox announcing an all-hands meeting that afternoon. As soon as the email arrives, a palpable feeling of somberness spreads over the room. Thanks to me, we all know what's coming. And I won't be surprised in the least when I'm one of the employees being let go. By now, Sherrie has probably scrawled the word *RAT* next to my name on her list.

Later, when everyone gathers for the meeting, I keep to myself and stay toward the back of the group. But I can only stare at my shoes for so long, and so eventually I look up—and, of course, my eyes find Luke. He's on the opposite side of the room. He's talking to Erin from Accounting. As I watch them, Erin tilts her head back and laughs at something Luke says, then places a hand on his arm.

I guess Luke is going to get what he wanted after all.

"Good afternoon, folks," says Sherrie, as she walks to the front of the room, her heels clicking forebodingly against the floor. Everyone immediately quiets down. "I know you're all probably anxious to find out what this meeting is about, so let's get right into it."

I close my eyes. I wait despondently for her to break the awful news. Part of me expects her to even start listing off names here and now.

I'll be the first to be called, of course.

"There's been some rumors going around," says Sherrie. "Now, I'm not sure how these rumors started. But rest assured, there's no truth to them. No one is losing their job."

A sigh of relief goes through the room. I open my eyes. Wait, what? But I saw—

"We are, however, doing some restructuring. But again, it will *not* entail layoffs, folks. We're just going to be shifting some things around. You may see yourself assigned to a new team in the following weeks, but no one is being let go. Are there any questions?"

Murmurs of understanding ripple through the group. A few hands shoot up into the air. As for me, I feel like an utter fool. I want to run out of the room. I want to hide behind the nearest potted ficus tree.

Most of all, I want to go back in time and stop myself from seeing that stupid piece of paper on Sherrie's desk.

Sherrie answers a few questions, tells us that more details will be forthcoming, and thanks everyone for coming to the meeting. As the group breaks up and people head back to their desks, lighthearted chatter fills the air. I know I should be relieved, too. But I only feel humiliated. Now I'm going to forever be known as the girl who cried layoffs.

I hurry back to my desk and drop into my chair. Even sitting down, though, I still feel so visible, and I lower the seat a little. Then a little more. Then all the way down. I look ridiculous now, but I don't even care. If I could, I would crawl under my desk.

Instead, desperately needing a distraction, I open up the vendor applications folder on the server. A new batch of them have just come in. I open the first one and look it over. The applicant, a woman based in Alaska, makes custom sterling silver jewelry; her specialty is hand-engraving portraits onto pendants. As I flip through the photos she submitted of her work, engraved couple after engraved couple smile tauntingly at me.

I close the application and mark it as rejected. Then, sighing, knowing that this is exactly the kind of product our customers go nuts for, I change the status to *under consideration* and drop it in the folder for the senior product buyers to review.

Later that afternoon, I get a call about the job that I interviewed for. I run like a maniac out into the stairwell to take it. Through my labored breathing, I hear an upbeat HR woman ask how my day is going, remark about how beautiful the weather is, and then cheerfully offer me the position.

"No need to give me an answer right now, of course," she says. "You're welcome to think it over for a few days."

I catch my breath. I thank her for the offer. I tell her that I don't need a few days—that the answer is yes. And then I hang up and make my way to Sherrie's office.

* * *

I TELL myself that it's for the best. The whole layoff blunder, I mean. Continuing to work at Artisanal Gifts would simply be too torturous, now that I've accepted my true feelings for Luke. In fact, I've decided that the best course of action is to pretend as if Luke doesn't even exist from here on out.

Immature, I know. But a hundred percent necessary.

A few days later, though, I'm at home after work when I get an email from Catherine. The subject line reads: *Hawaii Pics!* I open up the email and find a link from the portrait photographer. And below the link, Catherine has included a note about there being some great shots of Luke and myself.

I'm not in the mood to look through the photos, but I figure I should get it over with. If I don't look at them now, I'll never look at them. And I know that somehow Catherine will be able to tell.

I log into the client portal and click on the first thumbnail. When the photograph enlarges, it instantly transports me back to Hawaii. It's been less than a week, but it feels like the photograph is from ages ago. We all look happy. Behind us glows an obscenely beautiful sunset. Around us, palm tree fronds are frozen mid-wave.

One at a time, I click through the photos, giving a few seconds of attention to each one. There are a bunch of shots of all of us posing together, in various crops and angles. Then there are photos of individual couples, starting with Mom and Dad. There's one especially great shot with the two of them holding each other and laughing. The pictures of Catherine and Kenneth come next. After that are the ones of Luke and myself. I click through those faster, barely giving each one a glance.

God, there are *so many* photos. When is the torment going to end?

Finally, I reach it. The last photo. It's a candid shot of all of us: we'll all looking out at the ocean. All of us, that is, except for Luke. Instead of focusing on the water, Luke's eyes are on me. And he has this...*look* in his eyes. The longer I stare at the photograph, the longer I'm sure of it.

He has real feelings for me, too.

* * *

I CAN'T SLEEP that night. I toss and turn relentlessly in bed. And by the time I do finally fall asleep, it's almost four in the morning. I stay asleep for less than three hours before waking up again. I take a shower, dry my hair, force myself to eat something, put on a little make up. Not that any amount of under eye concealer will fix what I've got going on.

Then I get in my car and drive to Luke's.

Standing outside his building, I steady my shaking hand and press the buzzer to his apartment. Luke answers with a groggy, "Hello?"

"It's Emma," I say, leaning into the speaker. "Can I talk to you for a minute?"

There's a pause. "Um, okay. Come up, I guess."

He buzzes me in.

Upstairs, on his floor, I find his apartment door slightly ajar. I walk in and close it behind me. His apartment smells like shampoo and freshly brewed coffee.

Luke walks out of the kitchen holding a cup. "You couldn't have just called?"

"I wanted to talk to you in person."

"At seven in the morning."

"Yeah. Sorry about that. But I—I couldn't sleep last night, and—"

"It's fine," Luke says, sounding impatient. "What's up?"

"I need to apologize to you," I say. "Luke, I am

really, really sorry about what I said to you in Hawaii. I didn't mean it. I was putting up a shield."

I see the coldness retreat from his face. He sighs. "I acted like a jerk, too."

"I really did develop feelings for you, you know."

"You did, huh?" he asks. I see the corner of his mouth curl up. Just a little.

"What about you?" I ask, my heart rate picking up.

A length of silence passes between us. Finally, Luke says, "I developed feelings for you, too."

"Do you still feel that way?"

Luke's smile vanishes, and my stomach drops.

"Look, Emma," he says. "I'm sorry. But I think we've established that we aren't meant to be together."

"But that was a fake relationship. It wasn't real."

"I know, but...let's just let it be. Okay?" He runs a hand through his hair. "Breaking up the first time was bad enough. If we have to go through that again, and for real this time...I'm sorry. But I can't."

I almost say, "Okay, so we won't break up, then!" But then I realize how ridiculous that sounds. So I just stand there, not saying anything at all. In the kitchen, his coffee maker beeps.

"Fine," I say. "I get it. We can just be friends."

Luke's eyes drift from mine. "Right, um...I don't know if I can do that, either."

"What do you mean?"

"It'll be too hard."

I can't believe what he's saying. That's it? What,

just like that, we're never going to talk again? No. I can't let things end like this. Maybe if I tell him how I really feel—

I open my mouth, but I can't bring myself to tell him that I love him. It's too much.

"You don't know how much you mean to me," I say.

"I'm sorry," he says. "You mean a lot to me too, but... I can't."

Every bone in my body feels shattered.

"I'm going to go," I say, and turn away. But before I fully make it through his door, I turn around to say, "I accepted a job offer. Just so you know."

"Wait, what?" says Luke. "But the layoffs didn't happen."

"I guess it's time for me to move on anyway," I say.

21

THERE ARE a lot of good things about my new job. My commute is eight minutes shorter. All of my coworkers are perfectly pleasant. My desk is by a window that looks out toward the water. There are perks galore, like a free membership to the gym in the building, discounted coffee at the adjoining café, and an extra week's worth of vacation days. And, of course, the job itself is better than what I was doing before. Now, as a senior buyer for a small import company, it feels like the decisions I make effect actual change at work. I even have a small team of employees reporting to me—although, truth be told, they're so self-sufficient that I barely have to manage them.

Still, I miss things. I miss the familiarity of the old office. I miss the silly team building exercises. I even miss the wonky drawer on my desk. But most of all, I miss Luke. During my first few days at the new job, every time someone has introduced themself to me, I've wondered whether they'll end up being my closest friend here. I've wondered which of them—*if* any of them—will be my new Luke. Minus the mess, of course.

After I finish up my first week, though, I begin to settle in. As I gradually discover the quirks of the office —a bathroom stall with a sticky lock, a coworker who talks to the copier, a small group who sneak out for a cocktail lunch every Wednesday—it makes me feel more at home. And I do end up finding someone who I click with, a woman named Brenna from Accounts Payable. By the end of my second week, we've already eaten lunch out together twice. There's no comparable restaurant to Tasty Thai in the area. But the alternative options do just fine.

IT'S a Tuesday during the following week when I get a call from the front desk.

"Package just arrived for you," says Carrie, our receptionist.

"A package?" I ask, confused. "I didn't order anything."

"It looks like it's from...let's see...a company called Novelties?"

"I don't think it's for me," I say.

"Just come up and get it," says Carrie. "It's addressed to you, Emma."

I finish up what I'm doing and then head over to the

front desk. Carrie is on the phone, but she points to a small mountain of packages stacked nearby. I spot the one with my name on it and, after giving it a gentle shake, carry it back to my desk.

When I open it up, I find a desktop bowling game inside: a wooden alley shorter than my forearm, ten tiny pins, and one itty-bitty bowling ball.

I laugh quietly, still perplexed. I set the game on my desk and search through the tissue paper that it was packed in. In the bottom of the box, I find a printed invoice. But there's no sender name. No gift message.

The miniature size of the game *does* remind me of the miniature umbrella that Paige lent me, though. Maybe this is simply her way of continuing on our friendship. The other possibility is that Luke sent it to me. But it doesn't seem like something he would do. Lucinda is also a possibility, I guess. But it doesn't seem very like her, either.

I decide not to do anything about it yet. After playing a few frames—bowling strikes, of course—I find a good place for the game on my desk and go back to work.

And, to be honest, I don't think about the gift much after that. Not until the following day. Not until I get another call from Carrie, letting me know that there's another delivery for me at the front desk.

This time I don't object about not having ordered anything. I simply go up and get my package. It's smaller this time. It's a square box instead of a rectangular one. *FRAGILE* is printed at a diagonal across the box.

Inside, wrapped in bubble wrap, is a cat mug. Not the same cat mug as my old one, the one that went missing all those weeks ago. But it's a pretty adorable one nonetheless. On the side of the cup, a tortoiseshell cat gazes up at me mischievously. The handle of the cup is its tail.

Again, there's no gift message, no sender info. But I know now: it's Luke. It has to be, right? He's the only one I told about my cat mug going missing. But why did he send me a new one, and the bowling game? If he's trying to tell me something, I wish he would just tell me.

I do love the new mug, though.

The following day, when I get another call from Carrie, I'm not even a tiny bit surprised. But when I go up to the front desk, I *am* taken aback by how large the next package is. Slightly embarrassed, I wrap my arms around it and carry it away. At least it's not heavy. In fact, it's oddly light.

"What'd you get?" a coworker asks, grinning as I walk by.

"Um...it's a surprise," I say.

By the time I get back to my desk, I've collected the attention of several other coworkers, too. I shove the box under my desk and wait until they stop waiting for me to open it. Then, covertly, I bend down and open up the box.

Inside is approximately a million tiny packages of honey roasted nuts.

I stare at the contents of the box. Luke sent me nuts?

No. Wait. He didn't just send me nuts. He sent me *airline* nuts.

I'm about to send an email to Luke—an email that basically says thanks for all the gifts, but what gives?— when my work phone rings. It's the front desk again.

"Hey, Emma," says Carrie. "There's a Luke here to see you."

A Luke. As if there could ever be more than one.

I thank her and hang up.

As I head to the front desk, my heartbeat quickens. I squeeze my fingers into my palms as I round the last corner. Luke is standing in the middle of the lobby, waiting casually.

When I get closer to him, though, I can see the nervousness in his face.

"Hi," he says. "How are you?"

"Fine," I say. "You?"

"I've been okay."

"It's you, right? You're the one sending me those packages?"

He nods.

"Why?" I ask.

"I've been thinking about you. I wanted you to know."

I notice, then, that he's holding a bag of takeout. I get a delicious whiff of Thai food.

"Is that..." I ask.

"It is," he says, and smiles. "Have you eaten lunch yet?"

22

LUKE TAKES me to a little hidden-away park a few blocks from my building. There are a couple other people there, but it's still nice and private. It's so lush that it almost feels like we aren't even in the city anymore.

"Before we eat," says Luke, as we sit down, "I need to say something to you."

"Oh, that's how it is, huh?" I say, smirking. "You lure me out here with Thai food, and now you're going to deliver a monologue?"

Luke laughs. "That's one way of looking at it."

"I'm just teasing," I say. "Monologue away."

He shifts in his seat. "Well...I've been doing a lot of thinking these last couple weeks about everything that happened. And so much is clear to me now. I shouldn't have acted the way I did in Hawaii. I shouldn't have been using that stupid app on my phone. I know we didn't have a rule against it, but still, it wasn't cool of me."

"It's not your fault," I say. "We should have talked about what sleeping together meant."

Luke nods. "Okay. Maybe that's kind of on both of us. Regardless, I feel bad about it. But there's also the morning you came to my apartment, when I told you that I couldn't even handle being friends with you anymore. In the moment, I really did feel that way. I really did think it was for the best for us to go our separate ways. But now that you're no longer in my life...well, it's been awful, Emma. Really awful."

"It's been tough for me, too," I say.

"When I pulled away from you, I was just freaked out about how our friendship was changing. I wasn't ready for it yet. But I'm ready for it now. I know your feelings might have changed since we had that conversation in my apartment, and if they have, I guess I'll just have to deal with it. But I can't go any longer without telling you how I feel. I like you, Emma. A lot. A *lot* a lot." His face softens. "I might even love you."

My heart threatens to burst. "You might even love me?"

"It sure feels that way."

"Well," I say, my breath catching, "I might feel the same way about you."

He starts to move in closer to me. My heart hammers away. But I stop him. "What about Erin?"

Luke leans back. "Honestly, I was never *that* interested in Erin. It was a silly crush."

"You're not just saying that, are you?"

"I'm not. After we got back from Hawaii, I talked to her a few times, and...well, she's nice, but it made me realize how little I was into her after all." Then his face turns cautious. "What about Alex?"

I blush a little. "Um...remember when you accused me of sneaking glances at you all the time?"

Luke nods.

"Well...you were right. The whole Alex thing...I've realized that it was an excuse I gave myself. I told myself I liked him because I didn't want to face the truth. But it was you, Luke. I've always wanted you. I was just too afraid to admit it to myself."

Luke grins. "The truth comes out. So...are we doing this for real?"

I nod. And keep nodding. I don't stop until Luke kisses me—an intoxicating kiss that takes my breath away.

And once we start, I don't want to stop kissing Luke. I really, really don't want to stop. But...well...we *are* in public. And my stomach has started to growl. Loudly. Angrily. Threateningly.

We break apart and both laugh.

"Let's eat," says Luke.

"Let's," I say. I eye the bag of takeout sitting next to us. Tasty Thai's logo is imprinted on the bag. "Please tell me you got spring rolls."

Luke grins and says, "Seriously, Armstrong? Of course I did."

* * *

"A FAKE RELATIONSHIP?" asks Mom. "What are you talking about, Emma?"

It's a few weeks later, and I'm on the phone with my parents, pacing around my living room as I come clean to them about Luke and myself. Luke is here, too; these days, the man is a regular guest in my apartment. Today in particular, though, he's here for moral support. He knows everything I need to say to them.

I take a breath and explain it to my parents one more time. I tell them again how Luke and I weren't actually together, how he was just a friend, a coworker. How he does not, in fact, own a startup.

"I'm sorry we lied to you guys," I say. "I feel really guilty about it."

"You and Luke weren't actually together?" Mom says, letting it sink in. The disappointment in her voice has never sounded so potent.

"We weren't."

"And Luke's business…" Dad says. He sounds equally let down.

"Nonexistent," I say.

"But I don't understand," says Mom. "Why did you feel the need to make all of that up, Emma?"

Cue the stomach twist. Because that, right there, is the question that I've been dreading most.

I hesitate, looking over at Luke on the couch. Even though he can't hear the conversation, he nods encouragingly.

"I wanted you to be proud of me," I say into the phone. It's so difficult, but so relieving to finally say. "I wanted you to take my life seriously."

"We *are* proud of you, peanut," says Dad.

"Of course we are," says Mom. "Why would you ever think otherwise?"

"I mean...compared to Catherine..."

"Oh, Emma," says Mom. "We're proud of you and Catherine and Garrett equally. We *love* you equally. I'm so sorry if you've gotten a different impression than that."

I swallow. "But you're always praising her, Mom. You're always doing what she wants to do."

"Catherine and I have many things in common, that's all. It doesn't mean I favor her." Mom pauses. "You know, Emma, we would love it if you shared more about your life with us. Sometimes it feels like we hardly know you."

It stuns me to hear her say it. But she's right. I don't share very much with them.

Mom continues talking. "It seems like whenever we ask about your work, or your personal life, you change the subject. But...well, I guess we should make more of an effort, too. I see now how we've fallen into certain patterns. Patterns that are hard to break. It was never intentional, though. Please know that."

"Not at all," says Dad.

I take a moment to gather myself. Then I say, "The reason I don't share very much is that I feel inadequate when I do. I mean, take my job. I'm not exactly doing important work, am I?"

"What about all those people whose creations you've gotten more exposure for? You've helped changed their lives."

"I guess," I say. "But there's also...well...at my old job, I wasn't making very much money, you know. I'm earning more at my new job, but..."

"We would never care about that," says Dad.

"Of course not," says Mom.

"Okay," I say. I mean, it seems so obvious now that they wouldn't care. But it finally gets through to me when I hear them say it.

"I'm glad you told us how you feel, though," says Mom. "And thank you for telling us about you and Luke. I do have to admit something, though. I'm sad to hear that it wasn't real. We liked him."

"We did," says Dad.

With a sigh, Mom adds, "You two really did seem like a perfect fit for each other."

I glance over at Luke, who arches his eyebrows questioningly. A montage of the past few weeks whirls in my head: so many coffee breaks and meals and nights spent together. So many spring rolls.

"About that," I say, smiling at Luke as I talk. "The thing is, we actually *are* together now. For real this time."

In unison, Mom and Dad say, "You are?"

"Yeah. As it turns out, we realized that we actually do have real feelings for each other."

"Oh, that's *wonderful*, honey," says Mom. "That's really wonderful."

"He's not thinking of founding that startup, is he?" asks Dad. "We really could improve our marketing, you know."

"Sorry, Dad," I say, laughing. "I don't think so. I'll ask him, though."

"Is there anything else you have to tell us?" asks Mom.

"What? Like about work?"

"No. About you and Luke. Is there maybe a... proposal in the future?"

"*Mom*," I say, my cheeks warming up.

"I'm only asking," she says.

"Yeah, um. You know, I actually have to go. I'll talk to you guys later, okay?"

In perfect synchronization, as if they've planned it, they both sing out, "Tell Luke hello!"

After hanging up, I sink into the couch beside Luke and let all of the air out of my lungs.

"Sounds like it went okay?" Luke asks.

"It did. I feel so much better now," I say.

"Good," he says.

"I still have to tell Catherine, though. And Garrett."

"Not this minute, though, right?"

I give him a look. "Why? Do you have something else in mind?"

"I have a few things in mind," he says. He walks his fingers up my arm. "More than a few."

* * *

WHEN I CALL Garrett and tell him about the fake relationship, he just laughs, calls me nuts, and then we move on from the subject. When I tell Catherine about it, though, she claims that she knew something was up.

"You did not," I say.

"I did," she insists. "I had a feeling, Emma. I swear."

"Why you didn't say anything, then?"

"I almost did. I bit my tongue."

"I didn't know that was possible," I say, and we both laugh.

Ever since our post-fight conversation in Hawaii, things have been so much better between us. We still have our quibbles, but they're more lighthearted now. There's no longer that underlying tension weighing down every exchange.

As it turns out, being on good terms with my sister is so much more pleasant than the alternative.

Astonishing, I know.

* * *

SIX MONTHS to the day after we officially start dating for real, Luke and I go on a long weekend trip away. We stock up on snacks and books, fill up the tank in Luke's car, and drive out to a secluded cabin in the woods.

Thanks to rain and more rain, we don't leave the cabin for the first two days. We still enjoy ourselves, though. We laze around. We gorge on snacks. We roll in the proverbial hay. We read. We talk. We play Twenty Questions.

Actually, we weirdly get *really* into playing Twenty Questions. Like, so into it that we play it for hours on end.

And so, on the third day of our trip, when it's finally sunny out and we finally venture up a nearby hiking trail, when Luke stops and asks if he can ask me a question, I assume that he wants to play the game again.

"Hold on," I say, and take a drink of water. "Give me a second to think of something first."

But then I turn around, and Luke is down on one knee.

"Emma Joy Armstrong," says Luke. "Will you marry me?"

I audibly—loudly—gasp. I almost drop my water bottle. Above us, the chattering birds go silent.

"For real?" I choke out.

"For real," he says.

I say yes. Of *course* I say yes.

EPILOGUE

"OH MY GOD," says Catherine. "I can't *believe* this."

"What? What is it?" I ask. "Catherine, I can't see."

It's the day of the wedding, and I'm in the middle of getting my makeup done in the bridal suite of the Magnolia Hotel. Hearing the dire sound of Catherine's voice, I'm desperate to open my eyes and see what Catherine is freaking out about, but the makeup artist is applying eyeshadow to my lids.

Actually, come to think of it, she's been applying eyeshadow to my lids for ages now. Oh, God. What kind of monstrosity is she turning me into?

"Catherine?" I call out. "Hello? Talk to me, please."

"I mean, *look* at it," says Catherine from across the room. "It's hideous."

"I don't know if I would use the word *hideous*," says Mom.

"No, it is," says Catherine. "I can't let Emma wear this."

The makeup artist gives each of my eyelids one last swipe.

"Okay," she chirps. "You can open them now!"

Tentatively, I open my eyes, bracing myself for what I'm about to see. I'm already convinced that I'm going to look like the Bride of Chucky.

But to my pleasant surprise, my makeup looks good. Actually, it looks *great*. I still look like me, just...a better version of me.

"What do you think?" asks the makeup artist.

"It's perfect," I say. I sigh in relief and smile at her.

"Awesome," she says. "Now let me just set everything with finishing powder, and then you'll be good to go."

While the makeup artist sifts through her makeup organizer, I take the opportunity to look over my shoulder and see what Catherine and Mom are talking about. They're on the opposite side of the room, examining a veil. My veil. The veil that Catherine said she was going to surprise me with.

"Maybe we can pin them down like this?" says Mom. "Or trim them off?"

"Hey," I say. "What's going on?"

Catherine looks at me and sighs. "I'm so sorry, Emma. The veil I ordered for you looks nothing like the photo."

"Let me see it," I say. From where I'm sitting, I can't make it out in detail.

Catherine and Mom exchange looks.

"What?" I say. "It can't be that bad."

"May as well show her," says Mom.

"Okay," says Catherine, bringing it over. "But *please* remember that this wasn't what I thought I was picking out for you."

As Catherine carries it over, the veil's hideousness becomes apparent. It looks like it's made out of cheap tulle and ancient yellowed lace. And jutting out from the top are bent wires that look like antennae—with pompoms on top.

"Oh," I say.

"I'm so sorry," says Catherine.

"It's not your fault. Anyway, it's not like I *need* to wear a veil."

"You really don't," says Catherine. "Your hair's gorgeous. Your makeup, too."

"Oh! Thank you!" says the makeup artist, as if I'm a painting of hers that Catherine has complimented.

"Thanks, Catherine," I say. I smile at her reassuringly. "And seriously, it's okay."

At the makeup artist's request, I turn toward her again so that she can dust finishing powder over my face. And while my eyes are closed, there's a knock at the door. I hear Catherine go to answer it.

When I open my eyes, Paige is in the room.

"Happy Wedding Day!" she exclaims.

"Thanks, Paige," I say, surprised but not surprised to see her.

Paige's eyes drift to the veil in Catherine's hands. "Ooh! Gorgeous veil. I can't wait to see it on you, Emma."

"Actually," says Catherine, glancing at me, "Emma had a last minute change of heart. She's not going to wear it after all."

"Really?" says Paige. "Oh, but it's so pretty. I'd *love* to get married in one like that."

Catherine and I glance at each other.

"Do you want it, Paige?" I ask.

"No, no. I couldn't take your *veil*."

"But you should. I'm not wearing it. And if you like it so much..."

Paige smiles sheepishly at Catherine. "I'm not even engaged."

"You never know," I say. "You and Martin are pretty lovey-dovey."

"You should take it," says Catherine, holding it out to her.

Paige looks at it again and sighs dreamily. "Okay. If you insist."

She takes it from Catherine and places it on top of her head, then peers into the mirror that's in front of me. And the crazy thing is, it actually looks good on her. There's still no way it would look decent on me, but somehow, Paige pulls it off.

Paige removes the veil and wraps her arms around me.

"Good luck, Emma," she says. "I'm terribly happy for you."

"Thanks, Paige," I say, feeling touched. "And thanks for stopping by."

After Paige leaves, Catherine tells me that she's going to run out and check on a few things. As she steps out, I can't help but feel overcome with gratefulness for her. She's helped me so much with planning this wedding. I'd be a stressed-out calamity without her.

"How are you feeling?" asks Mom, coming over to me. She smooths a strand of my hair. "Nervous at all?"

"No. Not really," I say. "Just excited."

"Good. You look radiant, Emma."

"Thanks, Mom."

"I'm proud of you, sweetie. Not for getting married. But…just…for being you."

I give her a kiss on the cheek. "That's really sweet of you to say."

Mom helps me get into my dress. It's a fit-and-flare gown made out of the most spectacular lace, and it hugs me just right. When I first saw it hanging in the bridal shop, I thought, *No way. It's too glitzy. It's too much drama.* But as soon as I tried it on, I was in love.

And, for the record, I have definitely not been wearing it around my apartment for fun. What kind of lunatic would do that?

Just as Mom is securing the last of the clasps that run up my back, Catherine pops back into the room. Catherine is wearing a pretty lavender dress, and you'd never in a million years guess that she gave birth mere months ago. I say that admiringly, though—not bitterly. Not anymore.

"Ready, Em?" Catherine asks.

"Ready," I say.

"All right," she says, grinning at me. "Then let's get you married."

LUKE IS MORE handsome than a male model in his tux—although, if you ask me, he's pretty damn handsome in anything. What I love most, though, is the way he looks at me as I walk up the aisle. No look could express a more genuine love.

"Hey," he says, when I reach the altar. "You look *beautiful*."

"So do—I mean, you look really great, too."

He laughs. He takes my hands. And then he squeezes them in that way I know I'll never tire of.

Standing at the altar with Luke, everything else temporarily fades away. I'm aware of the officiant speaking, of the significance of his words, but all I can truly focus on is Luke. I get so lost in him that I miss my cue when it's time to exchange our vows.

"Sorry, what?" I say, and everyone in attendance laughs. Myself included. "Oh—right. Yes. I do."

Luke says his vows next ("Most *definitely* I do"),

after which the officiant says a few last words, and then, like that, we're married. As we kiss, I'm so overwhelmed with joy that I can't even imagine feeling happier. When we turn to face all of our friends and family, though, and everyone is whooping and cheering for us—well, my happiness, it runneth over.

And so, as overjoyed newlyweds, we mingle; we eat our fancy catered dinner; we kiss on command when people clink their knives against their glasses. And later, when the music starts up, we dance. I dance with Luke, I dance with my sister, I dance holding my adorable five-month-old niece on my hip (who, for the record, is the cutest little blueberry ever), I dance with Paige, who, as always, has some new dance moves to teach me. I take breaks from dancing only to use the bathroom—which is a whole orchestrated thing, thanks to the infantry of clasps on my dress—and to refuel with the sweet treats that our caterer has set out in the form of a dessert bar. Naturally, one of the many dessert options available are chocolate cupcakes, each topped with a toasted marshmallow.

They are, in a word, divine.

At some point later in the night—I've lost all track of time—I look across the dance floor and see that Luke is getting his ear talked off by one of his cousins. He's a nice guy, Luke's cousin, but my God can he talk. It's like he's going for a world record or something.

I make my way over to Luke and thread my arm through his.

"Hi," I say, and smile sweetly at Luke's cousin. "Do you mind if I steal my husband away?" *Husband*. Yeah. I like the way that sounds. Husband and wife. Luke and Emma. We *do* sound good together, don't we?

"Sure thing," says his cousin. "I'll catch up with you later, man. Congratulations again."

"Thank you so much," I say, and pull Luke away. I pull him all the way to the middle of the dance floor. The deejay is playing one of our favorite songs—*Take My Breath Away*—a song that we have both always loved but only recently realized we share an affection for.

Luke wraps his arms around my waist, pulling me in close, and I sling mine up around his shoulders.

"Thanks," he says. "I owe you one."

"Oh, we're still keeping track, huh?" I ask.

"Always and forever," he says.

ABOUT THE AUTHOR

Rachel Arnett is a romance writer with a heart-shaped funny bone. *Emma and Luke Are Totally Together* is her debut novel.

For totally fantastic updates from Rachel, sign up for her newsletter at:

www.rachelarnettauthor.com

Made in the USA
Coppell, TX
30 September 2021